"Get down!"
warning wer

Brynne hit the dirt and called, "Fergie, come."

Another whooshing sound and then an arrow struck the ground beside her.

"Down." The dog obeyed, and Brynne threw herself over Fergie.

"Stay here." Jace removed a pistol from his jacket and moved toward a large tree trunk.

"Good girl," Brynne whispered to her canine friend. The dog let out a small whimper. She knew Fergie was still on the missing teen's trail, and normally she wouldn't have pulled her off the task. "You did good, Fergie."

Brynne removed her gun from its holster and looked for Jace. He'd moved behind the tree, and now she couldn't see him. Seconds ticked by and then minutes. She needed to call her team.

With a push on her radio, she said, "I think our shooter has returned."

She waited for a reply, but there was none.

Something caught her eye. A small footprint. The teen must've come this way recently. She whispered, "Come," and continued on the girl's trail.

She didn't want to leave Jace, but if she knew anyone who was capable of taking care of himself, it was him...

Connie Queen has spent her life in Texas, where she met and married her high school sweetheart. Together they've raised eight children and are enjoying their grandchildren. Today, as an empty nester, Connie lives with her husband and her Great Dane, Nash, and is working on her next suspense novel.

Books by Connie Queen

Love Inspired Suspense

Visit the Author Profile page at LoveInspired.com.

SEARCHING FOR JUSTICE

CONNIE QUEEN

LOVE INSPIRED SUSPENSE
INSPIRATIONAL ROMANCE

LOVE INSPIRED® SUSPENSE
INSPIRATIONAL ROMANCE

ISBN-13: 978-1-335-98043-4

Searching for Justice

Copyright © 2025 by Connie Queen

Love Inspired
22 Adelaide St. West, 41st Floor
Toronto, Ontario M5H 4E3, Canada
www.LoveInspired.com

Printed in Lithuania

MIX
Paper | Supporting responsible forestry
FSC® C021394

Rejoicing in hope; patient in tribulation;
continuing instant in prayer.
—*Romans* 12:12

To my sisters.

I'm so grateful you're not scared to ask me
to tell you about the story I'm working on.
That takes a lot of guts.

Thank you for being there!

ONE

A shiver skittered down Brynne Taylor's spine as the headlights hit the old Victorian house that had once served as her foster home. Raindrops streaked across the windshield, and a gust of chilly wind hit the side of her Ford truck, causing it to shake. Dead grass blew along the barbwire fence row, making everything seem barren and cold.

Brynne hadn't been back since Child Protective Services removed her from the Mooneys' home, just three days after Carrie—her foster sister—had disappeared. Not a day went by that she didn't think about that night sixteen years ago. Guilt still weighed on her, and she wondered if the feeling would ever go away. It would be a relief if she could make up for what she didn't—couldn't—do years ago.

Her gaze took in the vast home. Rain at nighttime gave the structure an ominous appearance. The truck's headlights reflected from the upstairs windows, almost like a light was on. The room had been the one she had shared with Carrie and their younger foster sister, Tessa.

Maybe she shouldn't have come tonight, when no one was around, but she feared returning to the home tomorrow might cause her to freeze up or make a mistake when her team depended on her. She'd only been with the K-9 search-and-rescue unit for the Rockford County Sheriff's Department for ten months, and the need to prove her competence pulled at her more than it should. A text had come through tonight from Lieutenant Dotson after eight thirty about the missing sixteen-year-old girl. The last place the teen had been seen was at Brynne's old foster home.

Two teens had gone missing from the same place.

Coincidence? Maybe. Or maybe not.

Coldness touched Brynne's shoulder.

Fergie, her Saint Bernard K-9 partner, brushed her nose against her skin before resting her head on her shoulder.

Brynne smiled and ran her fingers through the soft hair. "Hey, girl. We're not getting out tonight. I just needed to see the old place before we meet the lieutenant and the other deputies in the morning."

Big brown eyes stared up at her, as if the canine understood. And maybe she did. The dog had been hers ever since she worked with a rescue unit in Denver. After an avalanche that almost took her and the canine's lives, Fergie was dismissed from duty and Brynne returned to Texas to work with the local sheriff's department, since she couldn't leave her partner behind. Sheriff Loughlin was glad to add them to their search-and-rescue unit, even if Saint Bernards were unusual work dogs due to the heat in the Lone Star State. Being that Fergie was cross-trained as a cadaver dog added to her list of assets. But it didn't help that her boss, Lieutenant Dotson, had made his reservations clear about having a Saint Bernard on the team. Brynne got the feeling if it was left up to the lieutenant, he would insist she find a new K-9 partner.

As she surveyed the house, she wondered if it was possible the missing girl was hiding in the house. She glanced back at the message sent to her phone with the girl's name. Reagan Hepburn. Sixteen years old with shoulder-length dark blond hair. Approximately five foot four inches and one hundred and five pounds. The picture supplied by the teen's mother showed a pretty girl with dimples dressed in a cheerleading outfit.

"Reagan, have you been up there?" She leaned forward to get a better vantage point.

Fergie whimpered and glanced at her.

"Give me a few minutes and then we'll go home." She patted her head.

The teen had told her mom she was going to her cousin's house for a couple of days, but then the mom's sister called to ask for a recipe. Once the sisters were talking, the mom inquired how Reagan was doing. That's when she learned her daughter had never shown up. After questioning the cousin, the teen admitted Reagan had gone to Hope Valley—the closest town to the Mooney home. Several people had seen Reagan around, and said she'd been asking about Carrie and was staying at Nina's Bed and Breakfast. The last time anyone had seen her was yesterday, when she had inquired about going to the Mooney home. According to the report, a couple of deputies had already checked the house.

What if the girl was staying in the house? Maybe she had hidden when the deputies came by. Had Reagan met someone there? And if so, who? Brynne didn't know why she'd be there, but why did teens do a lot of things? Carrie had been about the same age when she'd disappeared. Brynne wished she'd handled things differently back then. She never should've told Carrie she would keep her secret—not about the baby or about her surreptitious meetings.

The wind continued to blow against the side of the truck and through the trees, sending the bare limbs dancing. After sitting quietly, listening to the rain hitting the vehicle for a few minutes, Brynne's nerves had calmed a bit. Her gun rested in her belt holster, and she had Fergie with her. The

Saint Bernard was in no way an attack dog—she didn't have an aggressive bone in her body—but she would alert Brynne to trouble.

The last Brynne had heard, no one had lived in the home for the past few weeks. Hopefully, the department would have a briefing in the morning with more details about the case than had been in the text. The Mooneys had continued to live in the house for the last several years, but as they grew older, they didn't want the upkeep. They bought a quaint home on the edge of Hope Valley. If they had rented the place or if any of their kids moved in, she hadn't heard.

The door to the old barn blew open and slammed against the wall. Her breath hitched. The image of a metal pipe lying in a small pool of blood and a person in the shadows resurfaced in her memories like it was yesterday. Her heart raced and her leg muscles tightened. What happened to Carrie that night? The blood had to have been hers.

Relax. The need to get this over with and return home to get some sleep before the search in the morning tugged at her. She closed her eyes and drew a deep breath. She hadn't wanted to wait until the morning because she knew she and Fergie would be expected to check out the barn, along with the other outbuildings. It wasn't uncommon for Lieutenant Dotson to arrive early, and she didn't want to take the chance he'd interrupt her looking things over. How could she face her fears of the past with an audience of coworkers?

The constant pressure not to make a mistake was always there, parading in front of her, reminding her if she didn't want another failed relationship, another failed mission, she needed to deal with her anxiety now.

"I changed my mind." She grabbed the flashlight and the leash from the passenger seat and shrugged into her rain slicker. Cold February air slammed into her, sending goose bumps down her neck as she stepped out of the truck and opened the back door. "This won't take long. We're just going to look in the barn."

Fergie's tail slapped the seat in anticipation.

Brynne attached the leash to her harness. "Come."

The dog leaped to the muddy ground. Footprints were scattered everywhere, but that was probably from the deputies searching the place earlier. At least the dog made her not feel so alone. Seeing the old home made her want to check it out, too, but she could do that tomorrow if the search called for it. Right now, Brynne needed to overcome her terror of the barn. Fergie waited until she stepped toward the bulky structure. It was difficult to see in the rain, but the old trail that led from the house was still there, although fainter.

She shined the light to the ground, then back to the outbuildings. Now that she had made her way across the open space, she could see there were no vehicles under the carport. She kept an eye on the ground for shoe prints or anything to show Reagan had been here. But she saw nothing. Since the girl's car wasn't there, she wondered if the authorities had found it yet. The text from the sheriff's office had little information.

As she stepped to the large wooden door, it blew shut again, the banging causing her to flinch. Before she opened it, she glanced back at the house. Nothing moved except for the grass. Raindrops fell from the roof in a constant pelting.

She took a step inside. Even though the rain had been incessant for the past couple of hours, there was no lightning. No outside security lights. All was dark except for what the little flashlight illuminated.

Fergie stopped and turned to look at her. Brynne ran a hand across her wet fur. "It's okay, girl."

The canine put her nose to the ground and started across the dirt floor. Old hay lined the floor, and water dripped to the ground in a few places. No doubt, the strange odor gained Fergie's attention.

The door banged open again. Hating that the noise made her jump, Brynne found a piece of lumber and propped open the door to the outside, making certain the board was secured against the framing so it wouldn't fall.

She shined her light into all the corners, and even on top of the tack room.

Back when she and Carrie had lived here, the room had been filled with tools—mainly for gardening—and devices used to work on the equipment. Most of that stuff was gone now, with only an empty five-gallon bucket resting next to the wall and a few boxes stacked above the tack room. The Mooneys must've cleaned out everything when they moved into town, which made her wonder if the house was empty as well.

Something skittered in the corner, and Fergie's ears stood. Brynne allowed her partner more room on her leash as she continued exploring the room.

With a deep breath, she squeezed her eyes shut. *Just get this over with.*

She opened her eyes and allowed her gaze to land on the floor in front of the tack room. There was no blood. No deep, dark stains from years ago. Just dirt on top of a concrete slab. She stepped closer and continued to stare. Nothing to give a clue as to what had happened. Her mind went back to when she watched helplessly as Carrie delivered the baby in the middle of the night in the back of a pickup bed, so no one in the house would hear what was going on. Brynne tried to convince Carrie to drop the infant at a safe place, but her foster sister was afraid she would be identified, and persuaded Brynne to drop the baby girl at a fire station when she was just two hours old. Even though they were close, Carrie never confided in Brynne who the father was.

She'd been surprised when Carrie had the baby. Carrie had always been curvy but had dressed in sweats and loose clothes the previous months. It wasn't difficult considering it had been winter.

Three days after delivering the baby, on a Friday night, her foster parents and Tessa had been at her foster brother Ricky's football game and called to say their van had broken down and they would be late getting home. Carrie had stayed home "sick" for two days before returning to work at the diner in downtown Hope Valley and had to close that night, leaving Brynne at home by herself. On weekends, the diner stayed open until ten and Carrie would get home about forty minutes after that. Being that Carrie was seventeen, she had her own car and was planning to move out in a few months. Foster kids couldn't stay in foster homes after they turned eighteen, so this was something the Mooneys had tried to prepare Carrie for. During the summer, she had interned at an attorney's office so she could have a job that would pay her bills.

It had been after eleven when Carrie pulled into the drive, waking Brynne. Being that she had worked on the Mooneys' small ranch that day, Brynne was tired and had already gone to bed.

Dozing off and on, it had taken her a minute to realize Carrie hadn't come inside the house until she heard what sounded like a faraway scream. It might've been the cat, but the noise had roused Brynne out of bed. She'd gone downstairs calling Carrie's name. When Carrie didn't answer, she went outside. Carrie's car sat in the drive. There was a light on in the barn, so Brynne went to check it out. Carrie had a few boyfriends, and she wondered if she was meeting with someone. When Brynne stepped through the door, she called Carrie's name again. Something bumped the wall.

Panic had hit her when she spotted a pool of blood on the floor—the same place she was staring at right now. If only she had run for help. But, of course, she couldn't because someone had moved in the shadows and grabbed her from behind, dragging her into the tack room.

The person had yanked her hair, making her head snap back. A deep, rough voice said, "Don't tell anyone about seeing me. If you do, I'll know because I'll be watching. I'll not only hurt you, but I'll come for that little sister of yours."

Chills having nothing to do with the winter night ran down her spine as the memories flooded her. He'd threatened to hurt Tessa, who was just nine years old at the time.

Perhaps she shouldn't have come tonight. She didn't want to face her past in the morning in front of her coworkers, but maybe she should've talked to the sheriff. Step away from this case.

But could she really do that when a teenage girl needed her?

No, she couldn't. Brynne was an officer of the law, and her duty was to help people. She was trained. She wasn't a frightened kid anymore and would never be swayed from doing the right thing again.

"Come, Fergie. Let's go."

The dog had been sniffing the area behind the tack room. Fergie glanced up momentarily, then returned to the ground and let out a whimper.

"What is it, girl?"

The barn door crashed shut.

Brynne pointed the flashlight at the door, but it swung open again. The wind had picked up.

"Let's get out of here. Come."

The dog stared into the corner and barked sharply. Brynne knew something caught her interest, but being trained to follow commands, the canine stepped beside her. She took up the slack on the leash, and they moved for the open door.

A shadow moved.

Déjà vu slammed into her as footsteps came from behind her. Fergie went into a barking frenzy. Brynne slid her pistol from the holster and dropped the leash and flashlight so she could defend herself. Her gaze went behind her, toward the tack room as she held her weapon ready.

Suddenly, something struck her. Pain shot down her right arm, and her gun fell to the ground. A powerful arm went around her shoulder, dragging her back toward the middle of the room and away from freedom. She was tempted to yell at him to let her go, but that would be a waste of energy. Her heels dug into straw-filled dirt, and her hands clawed at his arm. She threw her hips back, trying to free herself of his grip, but her momentum propelled her backward and only made her fall into his body.

Fergie continued to bark and dance around the room. There was no doubt that if the dog wanted to cause damage to the attacker, she could, but her demeanor was too sweet and docile for that. She simply looked confused and upset.

"Get out of here, dog!" The man kicked toward Fergie but missed. He dragged Brynne out a side door and into the rain.

She could've yelled for Fergie to follow her, but she didn't want the man to harm her. Instead, she hollered, "Retreat."

Brynne could no longer see her partner, but she hoped Fergie would obey. After sustaining an injury while in Denver, Brynne had been working with her on the new command to back away about thirty feet if she was too close to danger.

The man released his grip, and she kicked out in a sweeping motion, connecting with his ankle. He growled and then slammed her against the outside barn wall. Her head crashed into the wooden planks and lights danced before her eyes.

"You shouldn't have returned!"

Her world spun, and she tripped over a prickly brush, barely retaining her balance. She tried to make out his identity, but it was too dark. Suddenly, she was swept off her feet and into his arms. She kicked and bucked in his grip. A familiar scent came to her, but she couldn't place it. Her head came up and slammed into his chin, causing him to curse. Then she was dropped into a coffin-sized container and a door slammed above her.

Somewhere in the distance, Fergie barked. Her heart constricted.

Even though she couldn't see, terror gripped her as she realized where she was—in the old chest freezer the Mooneys used for a worm compost bin. Old leaves, food matter and worms had thrived inside, but back then the door had been propped open.

She kicked upward with all her might, but the door didn't budge. Even as her brain shouted to conserve her oxygen, she knew she must escape. The area was confined, and she'd die from asphyxiation before her team arrived in the morning.

"Help me!" The effort was futile, but hysteria for survival kicked in. She didn't want to die tonight. "Please, someone help!"

Jace Jackson heard barking while he was tucking Huck into bed.

"That's a dog." The three-year-old's eyes grew large.

"Yeah, it is." He was surprised Huck heard, as far away as it sounded.

"Is it big?" His boy spoke in barely more than a whisper and clutched the covers in his hands.

Huck had loved dogs and never been afraid until several months ago, when one of Jace's high-school ranch hands had brought his Great Dane with him to work. The giant dog wasn't mean but had a lot of energy. In his excitement, the dog had knocked Huck to the ground and proceeded to lick him on the face, making it impossible for the boy to get up. Even though the ranch hand got his dog under control, Huck hadn't forgotten it. "I don't know what kind of dog it is," Jace replied to his son.

"Can I go see?" His son yanked back the covers. "He might be a baby dog."

"No." Jace chuckled and returned the blanket to the boy's chin. The dog didn't sound small, but sometimes the bark could be deceiving. He dabbed his finger on the tip of Huck's nose. "You need to get to sleep."

"Aw, Daddy."

Jace gave his son a kiss on his forehead and then stood. "If the dog is still around in the morning, I'll let you see him."

"Okay. If he's nice." The boy sunk deeper into the bed and his eyebrows narrowed in obvious disappointment. Huck had been asking for a dog ever since their fourteen-year-old collie, Buddy, had passed away eight months ago. The collie had been the best friend for Huck, which was the reason he hadn't been afraid of the Great Dane. Jace hoped he got over his fear soon.

"Sweet dreams. I'll see you in the morning." He left the door open and strode down the hall.

Occasionally, someone would drop off an unwanted pet in the country, and he hoped that wasn't the case tonight. Normally, he would wait until morning, but after receiving a call from the sheriff's department asking for permission to search his land for a missing person, he thought he'd check it out now.

He let his mom know what he was doing so she could keep an eye on Huck. Then he grabbed his gun, saddled Doo, his horse, and headed across the pasture between his place and the old Mooney place. If someone was there, he didn't want his pickup to alert them. The Appaloosa trotted across the open land. Even before he neared the barn, a dim light flashed from inside. Someone was there. Hopefully, the missing person had been found.

When he neared the pen, he tied off his horse to some sagebrush and slid from the saddle. The drizzle continued, running off the brim of his Stetson. Keeping in the shadows, he maneuvered across the yard and to the front of his barn. A large, furry dog wearing a K-9 vest and trailing a leash stood beside a 4x4 silver pickup. The searchers weren't scheduled to be here until the morning unless something had changed. Had they learned more about the missing teen? He glanced around but didn't see anyone, and it didn't appear anyone was sitting inside the vehicle. It wouldn't hurt to make certain. He'd never worked with the K-9 units, but he knew handlers didn't normally leave them alone. Being wary, he stuck out his hand and whispered, "Good dog."

The dog whimpered and sniffed his fingers in reply. She didn't appear aggressive. He whispered, "Where is your partner?"

Big brown eyes stared up at him, and her tail wagged.

A glance through the rain-streaked passenger window showed the cab was empty. Footprints were on the ground in the mud. It was dark, but it appeared some were larger than others. Several people?

"Hello. Is anyone here?" When there was no reply, he headed toward the barn. The door swung free, and he stepped inside. Everything appeared normal, but he checked out the tack room to be certain. Finding it empty, he stepped back into the doorway and stared at the truck. A handler would never leave his canine unattended. Even if the person needed to leave the dog, they would put it in the cab in its crate, not in the rain. And definitely not out in the open, where anyone could steal her.

His gaze went back to the house. No one had been in the home since the Mooneys moved to the edge of Hope Valley a few weeks ago. As he headed for the front wraparound porch, his mind told him he was wasting his time. No one should be here. There had to be a good reason, but he couldn't think of one at the moment.

The front door was locked, so he used the key hidden under the metal bumblebee decoration and let himself in. The electricity was still on, and he flipped on the lights as he walked through the downstairs. When nothing presented itself, he checked the upstairs. No one was there. Besides a thin layer of dust, everything was as they'd left it.

As he came back out of the house, his gaze landed on the poor dog. Jace wanted to ride back home, but what did he do with the dog? He couldn't leave her out here in the rain. "Hey, girl. Where's your owner?"

He picked up the leash. "Find your handler. Search."

The dog glanced up at him but didn't move.

Jace kneeled beside her and petted her wet fur, smoothing it back. Her vest had the sheriff's department K-9 printed on it but had no names engraved on it. "What's wrong? Where's your handler?"

She barked and then took off. Jace followed, giving her room. She raced behind the barn to the opposite side of where he'd tied his Appaloosa. The Saint Bernard put her nose to the ground and then ran in wide circles, like she was trying to get the scent. Whether it was her handler she was looking for, Jace didn't know, but the situation was strange, so he thought it best to follow.

Was it possible the officer had learned something about the missing person who was last seen in the area? Maybe.

The dog trotted toward the pasture and then around the side of the barn. A couple of trees lined this side and there was a rusty freezer between them. She barked and ran up to his horse and sniffed before moving on. After a few minutes, he didn't think the dog was on the scent of anything. Suddenly, the Saint Bernard looked toward the pasture and her ears went straight up as she stared across the horizon.

Jace shook his head and withdrew his cell phone out of his pocket. He didn't know what was going on, but the sheriff needed to know.

The dog jogged to the rusty freezer and barked. Jace ignored her until she planted herself in front of it, sat and then yipped. Had she found her target?

He hurried over. Something pounded from inside. Using the light from his cell phone, he shined it on the old appliance. Even though he'd never had one, he recognized the antique freezer with the locking door handle. He opened it and was surprised to find someone inside.

A lady shot to her feet. "Get back!"

He automatically threw his arm to protect himself. "I'm not going to hurt you."

Her gaze landed on him as she searched his features.

The dog barked, gaining her attention for a second, before she looked back at him. "Thank you."

"Are you alright? What were you doing in there?"

There was enough light from his phone that he made out a glare. There was something vaguely familiar about her.

"I can assure you I wasn't taking a nap!" Her eyes grew large with frustration. "Someone threw me in there."

He recognized the annoyance in the voice, and he squinted for a better look. Realization hit him. "Brynne? Brynne Taylor."

"Jace Jackson. I should've known."

He held out his hands to assist her, but she shoved his

hands away and climbed out. Jace couldn't believe it. He hadn't seen her in years. "Who threw you in there?"

"I—"

A gunshot blasted.

"Get down," he said. The dog hunched low beside Brynne. "Do you have a gun?"

"Our guy out there disarmed me."

"Come on," he whispered. He carried a rifle in his saddle in case of snakes or other dangers, but he hadn't expected trouble with humans. Staying low, he hurried across the open land as more shots were fired. He didn't know what weapon the shooter was using, but he hoped he was out of bullets.

He noted how Brynne stayed between the dog and the shooter. When they rounded the side of the barn, he trusted that the building offered them protection, if only for a few seconds. He slid the weapon from the sling and fired.

The booming sound caused his horse to skirt sideways, but the reins held. A shadow sprinted across the open field and disappeared into the brush.

Jace turned to Brynne. "Would you like to tell me what you're doing out here?"

She kneeled by the dog as if she was checking her for injuries. After a moment, she stood and planted a hand on her hip and angry, amber eyes stared back at him. Her brunette hair was plastered to her face and moisture ran down her cheeks. "There's a missing teen."

"And the searchers aren't supposed to be here until morning," he countered.

"Yeah, well, I came early." She glanced over her shoulder to where the man had vanished, then turned back to him. "Not only is there a missing sixteen-year-old girl out there, but also a gunman who'd like nothing more than to stop me from investigating. And if I want to stay alive, I need to figure out why."

TWO

Jace shook his head and said, "Come on. Let's get out of the rain, where we can talk, and I can call this in."

"I'll do it." Brynne grabbed Fergie's leash and followed her ex-crush around the barn to where she found her gun on the ground where she'd dropped it. Then she went to her vehicle. She grabbed a fresh towel from the floorboard, where she kept a stash to clean Fergie's paws. She straightened the rubber mat on the seat and patted it. "Kennel."

Her partner leaped onto the mat, and Brynne did as good as possible of getting the mud off her paws before allowing her in her safety crate. Then she swiped another towel and climbed into the front seat of her truck. She ran the towel through her hair and did the best she could to fluff it. Using her cell phone, she called the station to let them know what had happened.

"Sheriff's department."

"Hey, Allison. This is Brynne. I'd like to report a shooting." The dispatcher listened and took the information.

"Hey, isn't that the address of the Mooney place? Where the search is supposed to be in the morning for that missing girl?"

Brynne hated to admit she'd gone by the property early, but she couldn't very well hide that there had been a shooting, either. "Yes, that's correct."

"I'll send a send a deputy out. Randall is the closet to you."

"Thanks, Allison." After she disconnected, dread settled on her. The sheriff would not like her coming out here early. She rolled down her window.

Rain dripped off of the brim of Jace's hat. "You want to come by the ranch and talk about this?"

"No, thanks. I'll wait here. Do you want to get in?"

"Naw. I'm already wet and there's no need to get your passenger seat wet."

She glanced at the distance over the horizon, where his parents used to live. "Do you still live with your parents?"

His lips quirked at the corners. "No. Dad passed away several years ago. Mom moved to Mississippi to help take care of her mom and spend more time with her sisters before moving back here."

"I didn't know your dad died. I'm sorry to hear that." She truly was saddened to learn of his passing. Benjamin Jackson was a good man, and she knew Jace was close to him. But she had enough on her mind visiting the old home, and the last thing she wanted was to add Jace Jackson to the list of things that was cluttering her mind. "I'll go home tonight. It'll probably be after midnight by the time we're done."

His hand grabbed the top of the cab as he leaned against his arm, rain continually dripping from his cowboy hat. "Brynne, who was that guy that locked you in the freezer and then was shooting at you?"

She shrugged irritably. "I don't know. How could I? I assume it has something to do with Reagan Hepburn, the missing girl."

"You think you're safe to go back home. Do you have protection?"

"Of course, I do. I'm a deputy."

"I'm assuming you live alone. Maybe you are this guy's target."

Why did he assume she lived alone? She could have a husband and a kid or two. Him being right irked her. "I appreciate your concern. But I'm tired and have an early morning." She shot him a smile. "It was nice seeing you again."

His brown eyes swirled with emotion, and she could tell he was irritated. "You live in Pepper Creek. Right?"

"Yeah. How did you know?"

He shrugged. "Someone mentioned it. Don't remember who."

Hope Valley and Pepper Creek were small, country towns. It shouldn't surprise her, but it did after living in Denver. She'd been thirteen when she was moved to the Mooney foster home, and Jace had worked next door on his family's ranch. He also did projects for the Mooneys. Since he was four years older than her and extremely good-looking, she'd had the biggest crush on him. They'd never dated, per se, but they had spent many hours together working on the ranch. Brynne loved being outside and riding horses, and Jace had been sweet icing on the cake.

His gaze took her in before he sent her a nod. "I'll stick around until the deputy gets here."

"There's no need."

He frowned and didn't say a word, then turned and walked away. She watched until she saw the silhouette of him sitting atop a horse in this miserable night. But he didn't ride away. She should've known he would stay to watch over her. He'd always had a protective nature. Sadness, and maybe a little excitement, filled her at seeing him again. They had been close during a tough time for Brynne, when she'd been moved from her previous foster home. The young couple had no children of their own. When an infant boy was placed with them and became available for adoption, they decided to also adopt him and the three-year-old girl that was already in their care. Brynne had been the extra child they no longer needed to feel fulfilled as a family. Not that Brynne didn't understand—couples wanted babies, but it had hurt just the same.

The Mooneys cared for older children, many times until the child aged out of the system and moved out on their own. Brynne had taken to them instantly. Living in the country and working with animals had been a dream come true. Sharing a room with Carrie and Tessa had made her feel a part of a family, even more than before she was removed from her biological mom's house. They went to church and said a blessing before meals. The school in Hope Valley was small and seemed to take to the new foster kid. Jace had been a part of it all.

Until the night Carrie disappeared.

In one night, everything changed. *Everything.*

She never knew what had happened to Carrie that night. Had she survived? Brynne didn't think so, but she hated to give up hope.

Brynne had learned a hard lesson—never depend on anyone else. Be friendly. Get along. But don't put your future in the hands of others, because they could be ripped away in an instant. Her dependence on others suffered after her dad died and then her mom married an abusive man. Brynne was removed from her mom's house for medical neglect after her stepfather had struck her. Why her mom didn't do more to protect her, Brynne would never understand. The Mooneys had treated her as family, and Carrie had become an instant sister.

A whimper came from the back seat, and she looked at Fergie. "Except for you, girl. You've never let me down."

Jace's question came back to her. Who was the man in the barn?

You shouldn't have returned.

Was it possible the man tonight was the same as the one who was here the night Carrie disappeared? She hadn't got a look at him this time, either. An eerie feeling came over her. How did he know Brynne would be at the barn tonight? She had told no one.

Or was he here already, and she had interrupted him? She swallowed. Either way, this was not good.

Headlights shone on the road, and a minute later, Deputy Randall's truck pulled into the drive and stopped beside hers. He got out and walked over to her door. Brynne shared an office with the lawman. He was in his late twenties and had a pretty wife with two young kids at home. She rolled down her window and noticed Jace riding away. A cold gust blew through the cab.

"Hello, Brynne. What are you doing out here?" His concerned gaze went to Fergie in the back seat. "Are you searching for the missing girl already?"

She shook her head. "I wanted to get a look at the place but had no intention of working until the morning. Would you like to sit in my truck to get out of the rain while we talk?"

"No, thanks. It's not that bad. Tell me what happened."

Through the open window, she told him about Fergie seeing someone right before she was attacked, and then about being thrown into the freezer and Jace Jackson letting her out.

He let out a slow whistle. "You're fortunate Jace came along. You might have run out of air before morning. I imagine that was pretty scary. Hope you're not claustrophobic."

"I never have been, but a little more time locked in the freezer may have converted me. And, yeah, it was scary." She wasn't about to deny it. He was right. She didn't like to think about it. Was it the gunman's plan that she would suffocate before morning? When the search team showed up in the morning, would they have found her? Did the gunman realize she was part of the search-and-rescue team? Or had he simply followed her here?

"Allison said something about shots fired."

"Yeah." She explained about the shooter and told him where he had been located.

"Can you describe him?"

"Not really, but I'll try." She thought back to when he seized her in the barn. "I didn't get a look at his face, but he grabbed me from behind and felt bulky. I'd say he was of average height, and he wore jeans. His shoes were shiny, maybe boots. They looked dark, but maybe that's because they were wet." She shrugged.

"Anything else? The type of gun, headwear, glasses, color of his shirt?"

"Hopefully, you'll find casings on the ground. It sounded like a rifle, but if fired one shot at a time, not like an automatic rifle."

"Okay. Thanks. It's muddy out here, but I'm going to look around and make certain the man is gone." He waved as he headed back to his vehicle.

"Thank you." She waited inside her truck for the next fifteen minutes but kept a lookout in case the man came back. When Randall returned, he let her know he hadn't seen anyone, and hadn't found any bullet casings.

Afterward, as she went to leave, she saw Jace sitting on his horse in the distance. He didn't ride away until she pulled out onto the road. Even though things had been less than cordial when she last talked to him, she was glad to see him again. He had said—promised—they would always stay in contact with each other no matter what. He'd probably meant when he went to college and didn't realize she would be moved to a different foster home after Carrie disappeared. But when she texted him with her new address and he didn't respond, it had cut deep that he broke his word. When he finally called her two years later, she'd been cold to him.

Thirty minutes later, she reached her place on the edge of Pepper Creek, on the south side of Rockford County. Her two-bedroom white house was set back from a paved road about a mile from town. Most of her neighbors either lived in older homes or doublewides. Many had young children. Some single people might not enjoy living among young families, but Brynne did. It gave her a sense of community.

The rain had stopped, and her headlights shined against the house. Everything appeared as it had when she'd left. She let Fergie out of her crate. The dog was ready to go inside. For a Saint Bernard, she was in good physical shape and exercised regularly. Because of the hot Texas temperatures, Brynne kept her fur trimmed short in the summer.

After she fed Fergie, her furry friend lay down on her bed in the living room and watched as Brynne made herself a quick snack before she got ready for bed. She was exhausted, but if she wanted to sleep, she needed to unwind first.

She fell into her recliner and turned on the television but turned down the volume. Since she lived on a low income, she decorated the home with finds at estate sales or thrift stores. As a child, she'd moved from home to home, so it was important for her to make the house feel welcoming and comfortable—much like the Mooneys' place.

She pulled out an old photo album from under the coffee table and flipped it to the first page. It was a picture of her and Jace with Flash, a black horse she used to ride. Jace wore a baseball cap and jeans, and his smile, complete with two dimples, lit up his face.

Against her will, her heart felt lighter. He'd been her first crush. After she was sent away, she'd carried the photo with her at all times. She'd even taken a picture of it on her cell phone, so she'd always have it. It had got her through many a lonely night.

She drew a deep breath. She couldn't go back to the feelings for him. If she did, her life would be turned upside down and hope would return. Even though Jace and her hadn't dated, they had the promise of a relationship. He'd been her best friend and they'd spent their last summer together. They'd talk about the future, and it always included them being together. Phrases like, "when we," or "after I finish college, we'll buy so-and-so." As in when she was older... She'd been young, but she hadn't imagined the implied meaning. Their last Christmas together, he'd bought her a lab puppy. She had to leave Cocoa behind when she was moved. Nope. She couldn't do it again. Hope would make her vulnerable all over again, and her fate would lie in someone else's hands.

It was a chance she wasn't willing to take.

Jace unsaddled his horse and rubbed him down, then fed him. He shut the gate to his pen. "Good night, Doo."

As he strode to the house, he was aware of his surroundings and kept an eye out for the gunman. Jace had seen no vehicles, but the man must've driven something. He'd watched Deputy Randall drive by slowly several times before leaving for the night.

The bigger question was why was someone after Brynne and was she the actual target?

He couldn't believe that she had returned after all this time. He felt bad for the way things had ended years ago. They had made a pact that their relationship would continue no matter what happened in the future. In Jace's mind, he had never thought that Brynne would be moved from the Mooney foster home when he made the promise. With his parents' unrelenting urging, he'd finally made plans to go to college, after putting it off for three years after high school. Brynne had talked about her future plans to stay in the area and had mentioned several career ideas, even though she hadn't decided on anything. She had already gone through so much in her life, from losing her dad, to her mom marrying an abusive man, to being taken away and moved from home to home before being placed with the Mooneys. Sonny and Celine Mooney were a great couple and wonderful parents who took care of several foster kids over the years. The thing was, most of the time, children aged out of their house.

He hadn't dreamed Brynne would be moved before she turned eighteen. After she was gone, he was determined to find out where she moved and to pick back up where they left off. And he would have, too, if Sonny hadn't asked him not to. Her second night gone, she texted Jace her new address in Amarillo. He'd told her thanks and that he'd be in touch. Jace was sure he'd made a mistake not going to see her, but Sonny had told him he had seen these things happen in families, and it was very hard on the child to progress if the people from their past kept interfering. Sometimes it made teens run away, which began another series of problems, from being moved again to being put in juvenile detention. Sonny all but demanded that Jace keep his distance and give Brynne time to get to know her new family so she could put down roots. That if Jace cared for her, he would leave her alone.

Two years later, Jace discovered she'd moved from her foster home and joined the police academy. He tried to call, but she didn't answer, so he texted her and asked when a

good time was for him to visit. She told him she would holler if she found the time. That had been fourteen years ago.

Looking back, he wished he hadn't taken Sonny's advice.
He'd had nothing but respect for the man, making it impossible to go against him. It was one of Jace's biggest regrets.

After Brynne had left, he'd dated a couple of girls in college, but nothing serious. He received his bachelor's degree
in business management and then worked as a security business analyst for a biotechnology company. It wasn't a terrible
job, but wearing a tie and dress attire daily had never been
his thing and being indoors all day made him claustrophobic. He missed the ranch, the sun and the animals. When his
dad died of a heart attack, Jace realized life was short and it
was time to change his career path. Being content was better
than a large bank account. While still working, he bought
the ranch from his mom and purchased as much of the adjoining land as he could afford. After another year, he'd finally quit his corporate job, doubled the size of his herd and
began ranching full-time.

Jace had met a nurse named Maggie at the hospital when
one of Jace's ranch hands had broken his leg and needed sur-
gery after the ranch hand turned a tractor over, and the front
tire ran over his leg. Two days later, once the farmhand was
released, Jace and Maggie began dating. Not only did her
love for the country life remind him of Brynne, but she also
struggled with some of the same trust issues. They married
a year later. Soon, she began complaining about there not
being anything to do and would ask him to take her to Dallas. Living on the ranch and riding horses quickly bored her.

Eighteen months into their marriage, they had Huck,
which seemed to appease her temporarily. Before Huck's
first birthday, Maggie was killed in a car accident in a neigh-
boring county. Thing was, she was supposed to be at work.

Jace learned she had been having an affair with a coworker. In hindsight, he realized Maggie reminded him of Brynne with her friendly and fun personality, but his wife soon became bored with ranch life and marriage.

After being burned by love, Jace vowed to never make that mistake again.

Now that he had Huck, he needed someone who would stay, even in tough times.

He showered and dressed in clean clothes, but he didn't get ready for bed. There would be no sleep tonight. He packed a backpack full of food and then refilled his bag of ammunition. He loaded everything in his farm truck. No one faced violence or gunfire from the biotech company, but after working in security, he quickly learned the lengths people would go to be devious and to cover their tracks.

He drove across the back roads to the highway to Pepper Creek. Brynne wouldn't ask him to watch over her, but he wasn't about to leave her on her own. He had no idea who had targeted her, or if it was connected to Reagan Hepburn, but he was afraid Brynne might not comprehend the danger she was in.

THREE

Considering she'd gotten little sleep last night, Brynne was overflowing with anxious energy and was ready to get on the road. The meeting time was seven o'clock, but it was a little before six. Brynne had checked her SAR—search and rescue—backpack twice to make certain she had everything packed.

Clouds drowned out the pink of morning, promising another sunless day. She loaded her equipment, and Fergie leaped into the crate. Just like Brynne, the dog seemed ready for action. The drive gave her time to think about the search for Reagan. She tried to keep her mind off last night's events, but it seemed the guy kept returning to her thoughts.

When they pulled into the drive, there was an older pickup sitting there. Brynne was leery until she spotted Jace coming out of the barn.

She stepped out and let Fergie out of her crate. It always helped if both of them could warm up before a search. She was wearing her long-sleeved K-9 T-shirt, but had packed her Gore-Tex jacket just in case she needed it. By the look of the clouds, snow could be in their future. The forecast had called for a low chance of freezing precipitation, but it was difficult to predict Texas weather.

"Morning," Jace said, greeting her with a touch to the brim of his hat.

"What are you doing here?"

"I'm going to help with the search since the girl may be on my place."

Did she catch that right? "You own the Mooney place now?"

He shook his head. "Only part of it. Five years ago, I bought a hundred acres—it's all I could afford—and Mr. Mooney kept sixty, including the part the house sits on. They sold it to me because their kids have no interest in living in the boonies. Their description, not mine. A few months ago, someone else made an offer to buy the home when they decided to move." He shrugged. "The price was a little too steep for ranch land. I probably should've found a way."

She looked at the old house again. Sadness nipped at her. Even though it sort of looked like something out of a scary movie, Brynne liked the old home and thought it would be fun to fix up. "I've always loved the place."

He nodded. "It was nice once, but it needs a lot of work. I'd say it's the definition of a money pit."

"I'm sure you're right." Brynne had thought the home would look great painted a cheerful yellow with white trim. And the landscaping would need a lot of work, but she could easily picture the finished project. It shouted *home*. But she would never be able to afford anything like this on her budget. And besides, Jace said someone else had already bought it.

Something reflected in the distance before a couple of deputies' and Sheriff Loughlin's SUVs came into view. A maroon sedan pulled in behind them.

"Fergie, stay." Brynne walked over to the other deputies. Even though she had been with the department for over ten months, and everyone was nice, she still felt like the newcomer. Being that Fergie was a Saint Bernard in Texas also set her apart. She tried to shove it to the back of her mind and fought the urge to try to prove the dog's skills to other officers. The only thing that mattered was the sheriff who'd hired Brynne and her partner. Of course, pleasing Lieutenant Dotson, who was in charge of the K-9 units, was a different story. He hadn't been as pleased with having a Saint Bernard on his team, and even less so, after another team from San Angelo had applied with the department after Brynne secured a position. It was no secret Dotson preferred German shepherds or Belgian Malinois, but Rockford County only had enough in the budget for two K-9 teams. Since Deputy Randall's Malinois was on short-term medical leave because of a carpal hyperextension injury he'd gotten while training in rugged terrain, Jeff Mayes, and his dog, Boss, a German shepherd, was the other team called in from Pepper Creek Police Department. The lieutenant was cordial to Brynne, so maybe it was her imagination that he wanted her off the K-9 unit.

Then, there was a rumor Sheriff Loughlin was retiring at the end of the year. If that was true, would a new sheriff keep her on?

While the sheriff gathered things from his vehicle, Lieutenant Dotson and Deputy Randall walked over.

Randall said, "Looks like you didn't have any more trouble last night."

"No, I didn't. Are you pulling a double shift?"

"I am. But I don't mind. I could use the overtime. And looking for this girl is important. I know if my daughter was missing, I would want all hands on deck."

Dotson nodded. "I agree. My Leah is about Reagan's age. Is your Saint Bernard ready for what could be a long search?"

"She's ready." Brynne forced a smile and held back her defense of her partner. It was almost like the lieutenant wasn't familiar with Fergie's work. That wasn't true. Just last month during a three-day K-9 search-and-rescue retreat, her partner took fourth place among forty-three participants in a variety of tasks and challenges, even beating out the team from Cheyenne County that was the unofficial rival of Rockford County.

Brynne didn't believe the lieutenant didn't like Fergie, but rather he couldn't believe the breed was suitable for Texas.

After Carrie disappeared, Brynne could imagine all too well what it was like to have a teen go missing. She wouldn't wish that on her worst enemy. She walked back to Fergie as Jeff Mayes unloaded Boss from his car. She guessed the lieutenant had asked them for assistance on the case. She gave Jeff a wave.

Jace remained standing where he was and watched her.

Several more vehicles came down the road and pulled in. She recognized several from the community. Two ladies that had similar features to the missing girl, and one who looked to be a teen, climbed out of a Lexus. Brynne guessed they were Reagan's mom, aunt and cousin, who'd first realized Reagan was missing. Her heart went out to the family, and she prayed the girl would be found soon. It was always good to have support in a search effort as long there was no fear of danger. After last night, she wondered if it was smart to have searchers working beside law enforcement. Sheriff Loughlin called the volunteers into a group and explained their goals and how the search would be conducted.

She took Fergie's leash and led her around the place, from the front of the house to the barn, and ended at the shed. If her dog had any memory from the previous night, she didn't show it.

"If you don't mind, I'll stick with you." Jace had his hands shoved into his pockets. He was dressed in cowboy boots, jeans and a lined Western brush jacket.

"Don't get in my way."

One side of his mouth lifted. "I wouldn't think of it."

Her heart rate picked up as her nerves were on edge—she was ready to get started. Lieutenant Dotson gathered the deputies together. During the short briefing, he let them know the girl's car had been located at the Mooney home, but authorities had towed it back to the sheriff's evidence and impound yard so they could go through it and look for evidence. Deputy Davies spotted at least two sets of footprints, one leading to the pasture to the west. Fifteen minutes later, after the volunteers and law officers had been instructed and the dogs were given a shirt from the victim's suitcase that had been left at Nina's Bed and Breakfast, the sheriff yelled for them to begin.

Brynne gave Fergie time to smell the shirt, then she said, "Search."

Fergie put her nose to the ground and took off toward the house. She sniffed around the house and circled back to the pasture—the same direction the search team had gone. Brynne wore her light hiking boots because of the mud. Jeff and his partner ran a little faster, but Brynne held back. She veered a little to the left while Jeff went to the right, in the direction of Jace's property.

It had been years since she'd been on the ranch, and except for the vegetation changing, the land remained almost untouched. After several minutes, the two dogs began to go separate ways. Jeff and Boss moved fast and seemed to be on the scent, but Fergie worked her way through the saturated landscape, only occasionally seeming to be attracted to the scent. The twenty or so volunteers were spread about twenty feet apart and walked in rows. It didn't take long for them to get farther behind. She called over her shoulder to Jace, "You're keeping good pace."

"I'm not a total sloth."

Inwardly, she smiled. She'd known his pride would keep him from falling behind. For the next twenty minutes, they traveled seamlessly across the open pasture with little hint of detection. Had Reagan come this way? She was certain Fergie had picked up her scent close to the house. They came to a gulley and Fergie seemed interested. Brynne thought she might have caught the scent, but then she moved on.

"Something's bothering me," Jace said.

Without pausing, she called over her shoulder, "What's that?"

"If the girl has gotten lost, why was the gunman at the barn? Isn't it possible someone was after her? And maybe the gunman carried her in a vehicle to a different location?"

"That's always a possibility." And the more Brynne had thought about last night, the more she was certain the girl might be in more trouble than lost. During the briefing, Dotson had mentioned Brynne had been attacked, but quickly dismissed a connection to the teen.

Jace continued with his questions. "Why was the girl in the area?"

"She didn't tell her cousin why, but authorities believe she was looking for someone."

Jace stopped. "From the foster home?"

"Yeah. More than likely. Reagan had never lived with the Mooneys, but maybe she knew someone who did."

"Like Carrie? Carrie disappeared and now a girl is asking questions and looking for answers. Have you noticed that Reagan looks a lot like Carrie in the face?"

"I have. At least from the picture of her."

"That's a little more than a coincidence, don't you think."

They continued through the pasture. She felt like Jace was saying more. "What are you asking?"

She stared at him.

"I'm not certain." He ran his hand through his hair.

Brynne had never told anyone about the baby. And it had crossed her mind Reagan could be the infant Carrie delivered. But how could that be? No one could've known because Brynne had dropped the baby off at the fire station. No name or identification. "We can talk later, after we find Reagan."

They exchanged glances, and she figured he saw right through her. Was Reagan's resemblance to Carrie that obvious? Brynne had wondered if the thought had brought the similarities of their facial features to her mind. A lot of young girls had blonde hair and were slim. Carrie was a little curvier—something the boys had been attracted to.

The hill in front of her was steep and her boot slid in the mud, but she retained her balance.

"You okay?"

"I'm good. We hike a lot." The defensive words were out of her mouth before she had time to think. Jace hadn't accused her of not being fit. She and Fergie trained in many areas just like this. State parks, and all around where she lived. She tried to vary the landscape so both of them would be used to it. Fergie didn't slow down a bit.

"It's obvious you're in good physical shape."

Great. She wasn't fishing for compliments. She didn't glance at him or respond. He said the comment like it was a casual observation, but she didn't mind hearing it.

Lieutenant Dotson called in on the radio, and she let him know their location. She listened to the other handler give an update. No one had found a scent or signs of the girl since leaving the starting place.

He waited for her to get off the radio, then asked, "Is there any place you think we should look?"

"With all the rain, it's difficult to tell. Whatever tracks

and footprints were there have been washed away. It's possible someone picked her up in a vehicle and she's gone."
But Brynne prayed that was not so.

"That crossed my mind, too."

"But we've got to check out the property. Are there any
sheds or good hiding places that I may've forgotten?"

"I have three open sheds. Not much left of them, but I
suppose if you were trying to get out of the rain, they would
be better than nothing."

"Yeah. If you knew where you were going. That's just
the thing. Reagan wasn't from around here." Unless she was
being chased, why would she ask questions around town
about Carrie and then wander across open pastures? And all
the footprints have been washed away with last night's rain.

Fergie yelped with her nose to the ground.

Brynne glanced at Jace before she gave her partner more
room. After giving her a sniff of the shirt again, she commanded, "Search, Fergie."

The dog took off at a run, and Brynne hurried to keep
up. Jace was right behind her. The vegetation grew thicker
as they came to dense woods. They slowed a tad, but Fergie
was still on the scent. Brynne wanted to unleash her but the
last time that happened Fergie had gotten away from her and
gone down a steep mountainside. In the end, Fergie found the
six-year-old little girl and stayed with her for hours, keeping
her warm until she and the rescuers were able to get to them.
Brynne was determined to keep pace with her K-9 partner
this time.

Brynne took light, easy breaths as she continued to weave
her way through the thick brush. The hours of training had
paid off—she was both physically and mentally strong. After
several minutes, they slowed as the vegetation became almost impassable. She'd normally trim Fergie's fur not only

because of the heat, but also in times like this, when the briars and brambles get tangled in the long hair. She'd been putting off the trim until early March because of their chilly early morning runs. There were only a few weeks during the winter months in north Texas when the temperatures stayed below freezing, and even less often when they got snow or sleet.

Brynne glanced back to see Jace plowing his way through the brush. Instead of picking his way through the maze, he pushed or stepped right over various obstacles.

Something moved in the brush, nabbing Brynne's attention. A doe rushed through the undergrowth and disappeared. Fergie glanced the animal's way, only distracted for a moment, and then kept going.

"Is she still on the scent?" Jace only sounded a little winded.

"Yeah. I'm certain she is. Fergie's a good tracker." That was the truth. If she would've lost the trail, she would've given the indication by stopping or running back to Brynne. Movement flashed to the right.

She turned just as something went into the brush. Had Jeff and Boss moved toward them? Maybe they had veered off their path. To warn the other of their approach, she hollered, "K-9 team."

There was no answer, but she had to keep following her partner.

Whoosh. Something whizzed past her and hit the tree in front of her.

"Get down," Jace commanded as the warning went off in her brain.

She hit the dirt and called, "Fergie, come."

The Saint Bernard stopped and looked at her, then trotted to her.

Another whooshing sound and then an arrow stuck the ground beside her.

"Down." The dog obeyed, and Brynne threw herself over Fergie.

"Stay here." Jace removed a pistol from a hidden pocket in his jacket and moved behind a large tree trunk.

"Good girl," she whispered to her canine friend. The dog let out a small whimper. She knew Fergie was still on the teen's trail, and normally she wouldn't have pulled her off the task. "You did good, Fergie."

Brynne removed her gun from its holster and looked for Jace. He'd moved behind the tree, but now she couldn't see him. She continued to watch the place where he disappeared and in the direction the arrow had come from. Seconds ticked by and then minutes. She needed to call her team. After getting to her feet, she glanced down at her partner and put her finger to her lips. "Quiet."

With a push on her radio, she said, "I think our shooter has returned, but now he's using a bow and arrows."

She waited for a reply, but there was none. After another attempt, she figured trying it again was no use until she got to a better location. For now, she was on the move again. If this was the same man who had shot at them last night, why had he switched to arrows?

Was it because he didn't want to get the attention of the other deputies with the gunfire, and he didn't have a silencer? If that was true, maybe he hadn't planned the attack.

Something caught her eye. A footprint. Not large, like from a man's boot, but small, and it looked fresh. The teen must've come this way recently—after last night's rain. She whispered, "Come," and continued on the girl's trail.

She didn't want to leave Jace, but if she knew anyone that was capable of taking care of himself, it was him.

* * *

Jace silently weaved through the woods, the damp earth helping conceal his movements. The arrow had come from the northwest. He didn't know who this guy was, but he needed to be stopped so they could concentrate on finding the girl.

He'd played and hunted in these woods his whole life and knew them like the back of his hand. A half mile to a mile away, a rock road separated this property from the section on the other side of the road, but it was mainly pasture. That meant the attacker might have a vehicle parked along the road. More than likely, the man would stick to the cover of the trees...just like Jace would.

Jace stepped around the huge trunk of a pecan tree and spotted a boot print. He quickly followed the trail while keeping alert. Birds squawked and flew in the trees. Not knowing if the man was familiar with nature and the actions of animals, Jace had to assume he did.

A couple of minutes passed until a flash of black caught his attention. Jace paused and watched. A medium-built figure moved through the trees and quickly disappeared among the foliage.

Jace hurried to catch up. Noise sounded in front of him as the man clopped across branches, not appearing to try to be quiet. The commotion made him wonder if this guy was an amateur. Surely, professional hit men would not take a chance on being caught. The man moved faster than Jace anticipated and had put more distance between them. With only catching a glimpse of the figure, he still couldn't make out his identity. This area of Texas was sparsely populated, so if the man was from these parts, Jace would recognize him.

A dog barked in front of them.

That must be Fergie and Brynne. She had moved from their spot. What if they had found the girl? Jace must put a stop to the man now while warning Brynne so she would not give the girl's location away. And since Fergie had already made noise, he yelled, "Stop."

The man's steps faltered, but he kept moving.

Jace took off at a jog. He didn't want to interfere with law enforcement's pursuit, but he also couldn't chance the man getting away and finding Brynne or the teen. He weaved in and out of the brush, trying to make up ground. Just because the man used a bow and arrow didn't mean he also couldn't be carrying a gun. Occasionally, Jace spotted boot prints and knew he was going the right way. Suddenly, the prints came out of the trees and continued through the pasture. A quick survey told him the man must be running, because he wasn't in sight.

To the right, another dog barked. Several men appeared over the horizon, one being from the K-9 unit. Jace raised his hand to gain their attention and hurried their way.

When he got close enough for them to hear, he yelled, "The gunman from last night went that way."

Two deputies and the dog took off broke away in pursuit. When Lieutenant Dotson came up, Jace quickly filled him on the man shooting arrows and where he'd last seen Brynne.

"Are Taylor and the Bernard still on the girl's trail?" Dotson asked the question like he was doubtful.

"Yes, I believe so."

The lieutenant gave him a nod and kept going across the pasture at a fast pace.

Jace watched him. There was something he didn't like

about the way man questioned him about Brynne. Did the officer hope she failed? That didn't add up.

Somewhere in the distance, an engine sounded and faded away.

He hoped that wasn't the gunman getting away, but in his gut, Jace knew that's exactly what had happened. Who was this guy? And why did he have it in for Brynne?

He prayed she and her dog had found the girl by now.

FOUR

Brynne came upon a steep gully and had to slow. Fergie kept going, and she released her leash. Her partner trotted down the sharp incline to the bottom and disappeared. Brynne went down on her haunches and allowed her shoes to slide down the embankment while her hand dug the ground behind her. Her right boot slipped, and she went down on her bottom before reaching the base. She quickly climbed to her feet. There was no sign of her dog.

"Where are you, Fergie?"

The dog barked, and Brynne jogged to meet her.

After a couple of minutes, she felt like she'd gone too far. This time when she called her name, the bark was from behind her. She backtracked into the ravine until she saw pawprints in the mud and followed them. A deep indention presented itself in the side of the ravine wall, creating a cave-like space. All she could see was Fergie's tail wagging.

When Brynne got to the enclosure, her gaze landed on the missing teen curled up and lying on her side. She wasn't moving.

"Good girl." She reached into her bag and gave Fergie her favorite reward—a purple tennis ball on a multicolored rope. If Brynne had more time, she would've played tug-of-war with her, but that would have to wait. Fergie proudly took the toy in her jaws and her big brown eyes waited expectantly for Brynne to play. Finally, Brynne snagged the ball and tossed it. Fergie caught it and happily lay down on the ground.

Reagan had found shelter out of the freezing rain, but something wasn't right. Brynne went down on her knees beside her and wrapped her fingers around her wrist. Cold seeped into her touch, but there was a slight pulse. A rip marred the girl's jeans and her hair dangled across her face. When Brynne gently moved back her hair, her gaze landed on an ugly bruise that ran across her forehead, but it didn't appear serious enough to cause her to be unconscious. A gash cut across the middle of the injury, but it looked more like it had been caused by a hit to the head.

"Reagan," she whispered. There wasn't a response. She didn't want to move her without knowing the extent of her injuries. At first, she'd thought her hair was matted because of the rain and mud, but now she realized dark red clumped the hair. Brynne leaned closer. A large knot sat on the the back of her head. "We're going to get you help."

Brynne noticed Fergie had stopped chewing to watch her. "She'll be alright, girl. You did good. Now, let me see if I can get some help out here." She climbed to her feet and tried to call her team again, but there was no connection. Maybe if she got out to higher ground. As she heaved herself up, she wondered about Jace. Why hadn't he returned? She prayed he was alright.

She scaled the side of the ravine back to the top. This time when she tried, static sounded, and a voice came back. She still couldn't understand, so she climbed a little farther.

Finally, Dotson answered, "Did you find the girl?"

"I did. But she's hurt. Looks like she's been hit in the head, but she's alive. We'll need paramedics."

"Keep your GPS on."

"It's on. And Jace Jackson went looking for the gunman, so be careful." Even though she knew her team wouldn't shoot without identifying their target, the warning came unbidden. After she ended the conversation, she began to worry about Jace. If he was okay, he would've been looking and found her by now.

She hurried back to the enclosure and found Fergie had moved next to Reagan. The canine's brown eyes stared up at her as she approached. "Good girl, Fergie."

The dog had done this exact thing outside of Denver. There had been an avalanche in the Rocky Mountains and an eleven-year-old had gotten separated from his father. His leg had been broken during the rush of falling snow and ice, and he couldn't climb out of his location. He'd been pressed up against a large rock that he was able to use for shelter from the wind. Fergie had taken off down the dangerous embankment and found the boy. Brynne had slipped and fallen, twisting her ankle, and couldn't make it down immediately. Several hours passed before she worked out a safer route and found the two in freezing conditions. Fergie had wrapped herself around the boy. Miles, a rescue worker, was able to secure the boy on his snowmobile and get him back to safety. With pure determination, Brynne had gotten Fergie on her shoulders and carried her out, then they were picked up by another team member.

When Fergie was on her way down, Brynne wanted her to retreat, but she was already too far down the hill. This was why she'd been working with her to retreat to a secure location.

She sat next to Fergie, but where she still had a good view of the ravine. If the shooter approached, she would be alerted. Another look to their victim, and her heart constricted. Reagan reminded her so much of Carrie, but maybe that was simply because they were close to the same age as when Carrie disappeared, and both had blonde long hair.

Reagan must've learned her biological mom's identity. DNA tests were common nowadays. Brynne had left the infant wrapped in a blanket on the doorstep of the fire department. After a quick knock on the door, Brynne had run for the cover of the corner of the building. Seconds later, the door opened, and a firefighter stepped out. He'd glanced around while another person picked up the baby. Brynne had taken off for fear of being spotted.

Minutes went by. Birds chirped in the trees and a breeze blew. She listened for Jace or one of the rescuers, but heard nothing. Anxiousness caused her to hate sitting still. She got back to her feet and climbed the ravine again, careful to stay low.

Two squirrels chased each other before running up a tree.

Somewhere in the distance, something moved. She listened, trying to figure out if it was an animal. As it moved around, she realized it was much too heavy to be a squirrel or even a coyote. Bears were extremely rare in this area. Rustling came from the brush, and she eased lower. If she ran back down to Reagan, she might lead the shooter to the teen and Fergie. She didn't want to do that.

Instead, she moved along the ravine's edge, and ran along the top, just barely out of sight. A huge cedar tree stood about twenty yards away, and she dashed to it. The bottom branches were strong enough to hold her weight, and she quickly climbed the limbs, careful to stay on the back side, out of sight. Once she was three quarters of the way to the top, she stopped because the limbs were becoming too flimsy. Fergie looked up at her from the ravine. Brynne held up her palm—the signal for her to stay.

The shooter moved into view. He was wearing a baseball cap low on his head and a gray shirt, but she couldn't make out his face. He looked at the ground and seemed to be following footprints. Careful not to move too quickly, she removed her gun from the holster. She made certain her footing was sure.

A dog barked in the distance.

Brynne looked over the horizon to see three deputies making their way through the trees. Jace was with them. The gunman looked their way, but then disappeared into the trees.

"That way," Brynne shouted while pointing north.

Jace glanced up at her. The deputies took off in pursuit. She hurried to climb down. Jace was waiting for her. Brynne asked him. "Did you see him?"

"I saw him earlier, but then lost him. That's when the deputies came up. We followed your trail."

She was happy they had shown up when they did. "Come on. Reagan is this way."

Jace followed her into the ravine. "That's a great makeshift shelter."

"Yeah. It should've kept her dry. I'm assuming she found this place after she was injured."

Jace kneeled beside her and looked her over. "I'm guessing you're right. Looks like she lost a decent amount of blood."

Brynne nodded but remained silent. "It concerns me she hasn't regained consciousness."

He sighed. "We need the paramedics to get down here quickly. Minutes can make a difference." He turned his attention to the dog. "Fergie found the teen?"

"She did."

The Saint Bernard's tail slapped the ground.

Anticipation wore on Brynne's nerves. She had hoped

the teen could answer questions when they found her, but it looked like she would have to be patient a little longer.

"Deputy Taylor."

Brynne recognized the sheriff's voice, and she climbed out of the embankment. "Over here."

The man was fit for an old man and made his way over. He glanced in the gully, and when he saw Fergie, he gave a head nod. "Your team did good."

Her eyebrows lifted. "Even for a Saint Bernard?"

He nodded again. "Yep. But she's good at her job no matter the breed. Care flight is on the way."

No sooner had the words been spoken when a whirling in the distance sounded. She looked up to see a white-and-red helicopter appear over the treetops. "Come, Fergie."

The dog turned to look at Reagan like she didn't want to leave her side, but when Brynne called again, the dog came running.

Jace stood with her while the paramedics went into the ravine. Lieutenant Dotson returned with two other deputies.

"Did you find our man?" Jace asked.

Dotson shook his head. "I'm afraid not. Boss was on his trail, but then we heard an engine and lost him again."

Jace said, "There's a road to the west. He probably had something stashed over there."

Dotson agreed with a nod, then walked over to the sheriff.

She watched the lieutenant and wondered if he would acknowledge Fergie's ability. If Dotson was just another deputy, she wouldn't care. But he had the power to affect her and her K-9's future.

Deputy Randall glanced back at the lieutenant, then he stepped closer. "Taylor, you and Fergie did a great job. But I must warn you, Dotson's been talking."

"To who? About what?"

"He keeps talking about the German shepherd, Boss. I'm glad Fergie was the one to find the teen. I don't know if you're aware, but he and Jeff Mayes went to high school together. Dotson is always bragging how good Boss is at bringing down the bad guy."

"Fergie isn't trained to apprehend. She's strictly SAR and cadaver." Brynne struggled to keep her voice down. "This is what she was hired to do."

"I know. That's why I'm telling you." Randall turned around and made his way back to the others.

She knew it! If their positions at the department were eliminated, Brynne didn't know where else she might go. She wanted to put down roots, and Hope Valley was as good as any place she had lived.

Unintentionally, her gaze went to Jace. He must've felt her watching him, since his eyes connected with hers. When she realized what she'd done, she quickly turned her attention to Fergie and rubbed her back.

This area had always felt like home. But there were things that needed to be worked out. First, she needed to find out if Reagan was Carrie's child, and what had happened to Carrie. Second, when this was over, she needed to talk with Jace to make certain they had an understanding about their relationship—just as soon as she knew what she wanted to say.

Jace waited until the care flight had left with Reagan. He half listened to the deputies talk, including Brynne. She seemed on edge, not that he blamed her. From what he had picked up, the deputies were still in search of the shooter and would be talking with neighbors to see if anyone had seen a vehicle, including any kind of ATV. Jace knew enough about the area to know there were few residents.

Except for when he was at college and had the biotech

job, he'd lived here all of his life. They were on the outskirts of town in the corner of the county. Hope Valley was about fifteen miles away, and if it wasn't for the few farms and ranches, it wouldn't be large enough to have the one grocery store and three restaurants. The area was spaced out and sparse. Not that he minded. He preferred country life, unless something like this happened. The Hope Valley Police Department employed four officers. The county had more deputies because of the larger town of Bridgton, where the county courthouse was located.

Jace had assisted in a case years ago, when he loaned out his horses to the sheriff's department for a manhunt. Law enforcement tended not to use them very often nowadays. He watched Brynne with Fergie, and felt she'd found a career that suited her. Over the years, he'd often wondered what had become of her. Not being on social media, it was easy to lose track of those raised in the area. The couple of times he'd been on his sister-in-law's computer, he'd looked up Brynne, but to no avail.

When the deputies headed back toward the Mooney place, he followed at a distance. Brynne talked with Dotson and then hung back until he caught up.

She said, "Thank you for your help."

"I don't mind. You know that."

"I do. But I still appreciate it." Fergie walked between them.

He wanted to dive into the middle of the case and help her. She was too proud to ask for assistance, but he worried about her. His thoughts went to Huck, and he reminded himself he also needed to keep himself safe. He had responsibilities as a father now. "You can come by the ranch."

She glanced at him, shooting him a quick smile. "No, thanks. I need to go to the office. I'd like to help find the shooter. Or maybe go to the hospital and wait for Reagan to come around."

"Did the paramedics give an idea of when she might come to?" It crossed his mind that she might not wake up, but he didn't say it.

"No. They were still doing assessments. The main thing is to get her to the closest trauma unit."

Jace had figured that. "I will keep my eye out for any strange vehicles and let the sheriff know if I see anyone I don't recognize." He waited for her to say he could contact her, but she didn't offer.

"The Mooneys still own the house, don't they?" She looked at him. "I'd like to go through it."

"Mr. Mooney has already given consent to the sheriff and the deputies already searched it for Reagan, so I'm assuming you already have permission."

"Are their things still inside?" she asked.

"A lot of them, yeah. The home they moved into is a two-bedroom, and the rooms are smaller. I believe their kids are going to have an estate sale before they close on the house, even though the new owner said they could leave it."

"But the kids wanted to go through it? I never got to know Butch and Brenda very well. They only came around at Christmas."

"Yeah." He shrugged. "They're busy with their own lives now. Butch retired from the army and settled in South Carolina, and Brenda married a guy from Colorado, where they own a real-estate company. There are still some things they want, probably for sentimental reasons, and I'm supposing they could get money for the furniture. I agreed to keep an eye on the place since no one else is around."

Brynne asked, "But you have never seen Reagan before?"

He shook his head. "It wasn't until after the deputies found her abandoned car that they called me. Wanted to know if I'd seen her around or if she stopped by my ranch. I had heard Milly at the diner talk about someone new being in town, but you know how she likes to talk."

"I do." She laughed. "I miss her."

Jace glanced her way and noted the wistfulness in her eyes and the smile that lit up her face. "I'm sure she'd love to see you."

"I might later."

"Why did you come back?" He'd missed her, too, but didn't say it.

She turned sharply to him. Anger tugged at the corners of her mouth. "Why shouldn't I?"

Jace stopped walking. "I didn't mean anything by that. How long have you been back? A year?"

"Ten months. That's when I was hired by the sheriff's department."

He wanted to press more. Ask her why. Why she hadn't been by to see the Mooneys. According to Brynne, after she was taken away by CPS, her mom and stepdad had moved to south Texas—not that she probably had any desire to see them again. And she hadn't come by to see him. Again, why? Had he meant less to her than he'd imagined? That hurt more than it should. "I'll walk you through the house."

"I just want to make certain Reagan hadn't been there."

He asked, "You hoping she left some clue or evidence as to why she was there?"

"I know it's a long shot, but yeah." She wrapped her arms around herself. "It's getting colder."

It had been even cooler earlier, but then they had been hurrying across the pasture and woods, which kept them warm. His cell phone rang, and he saw it was his mom's number, so he answered. "Everything okay?"

"I was just checking on you to see how the search was going. Huck saw a helicopter, which, of course, got him very excited."

Jace smiled. His son was very observant. At times, it could be exhausting, but Jace couldn't be prouder. "We found the missing teen. She's injured and being transported to the hospital by care flight."

"Oh, no, I'll pray that her injuries aren't too serious, but it's a relief she was found. I was worried."

"We'll see." He decided not to tell her the teen was unconscious to avoid more worry. There were other things for his mom to be concerned with. "The suspect still hasn't been apprehended. I'd like you to stay in the house and keep the doors locked if possible. I know Huck is not going to like staying indoors."

"Oh, Jace. I don't like the sound of that." His mom let out a sigh. "I will bring Huck's farm set into the living room so he can play. We'll be fine."

His mom tended to worry, but she also had sense. Always had. "Okay. Let me know if you see anything suspicious."

"I will. Honey, be careful."

When Jace disconnected, he noticed Brynne watching him.

"Is Huck your dog?" Her eyebrows arched with the question. "Let me guess, a cow dog."

She didn't realize he had a son. There'd be no reason for her to know since she hadn't kept track of him. "Huck is my little boy."

She frowned. "I didn't know you had kids."

"Just one." He held up a finger. "He's quite the handful."

"Oh. Congratulations." Her chin dipped down and an awkward smile spread across her lips. Her voice dropped to a whisper. "Then that must've been your wife on the call. I'm happy for you, Jace. You deserve a good family. I always knew you'd find the right woman someday."

He looked at her, but she glanced into the distance. "Brynne, I'm a widower. Maggie died two years ago." There was no need to mention their marriage had problems or that Maggie was having an affair before she died. It probably shouldn't, but it made him feel like a failure that he hadn't been able to make his wife content in their marriage. Huck had been the best thing that had come from the relationship.

"I'm sorry." Her eyebrows drew together. "I had no idea. How old is your boy?"

"He's three and will turn four in a couple of months."

"That's a little younger than I was when my dad was killed." She stared down at her hands. "I'm sure you're a wonderful father. I'd like to meet him some..."

Her expression took on a faraway look, but he could make out what she was thinking. It had taken forever to get her to open up to him when they were younger, but once he got to know her, she was an open book. He guessed she'd changed her mind about wanting to meet Huck, which meant after the case was solved, she didn't plan to see him anymore.

She used to talk about her dad sometimes, mainly wondering how different her life would've been if he hadn't died. If Jace remembered correctly, he'd died in a car wreck when she was seven. If her mom hadn't married her stepdad, Brynne would've never been put into foster care—and he wouldn't have met her.

When they got back to the barn, where they had parked their vehicles, the sheriff was waiting for her and told her to come by the station.

Jace offered to give her a quick tour of the place, but she said she'd holler later, maybe after she met with the sheriff. He didn't like the distance between them. After dealing with Maggie and learning he hadn't known her as well as he'd believed, he felt like they needed closure. "We need to talk, Brynne."

"Later." She quickly loaded Fergie into her pickup and then she pulled out of the drive. What was wrong with her? Why the chip on her shoulder? Was it because he'd waited over two years before he tried to reconnect? He never would've done that except he wanted to give her time to adjust to her new foster home. If she would've just talked with him when he called her, he was sure they could've worked things out.

Brynne had been a natural around the animals. As he watched her truck disappear up the road, he admitted he missed that about her. Working with search-and-rescue had seemed the perfect choice. After everyone was gone, he got into his truck and drove around the expansive country block. He checked out the rock road but didn't see anyone around. Then he went by the ranch to make certain his mom and Huck were okay. Once he was satisfied that they were safe, he headed into town and drove by the sheriff's department. He didn't like that the teen had been hurt on his place. It was obvious someone wanted her out of the way, and that same person wanted Brynne dead. If Brynne thought he was going to sit back and watch it happen, she was wrong.

FIVE

Through the conference-room window of their small department, Brynne watched Jace's truck drive by. She couldn't believe he'd been married and had a son. She should be happy for him, but jealousy nipped at her. Why shouldn't he get married?

Because she had pictured them married and having kids. As silly as it was, she had thought she would be his wife. She couldn't blame Jace since she didn't live in the area anymore. What was he supposed to do? Chase her down and proclaim his love? It would've been nice.

He was a good guy and deserved his happiness. His wife's name was Maggie. Brynne hadn't known anyone by that name. That was a good thing, right?

Whining or complaining wasn't becoming and didn't benefit anything, so she refrained. Some people had tougher lives than others. It was just the way things were. You had to make the best with the cards you were dealt.

It surprised her she had brought up her dad to him. Jace had been the only person she had discussed her dad, Zander Taylor, with, and after all these years, she'd done it again. What was there about the cowboy that made her open up? It probably had to do with Jace's son losing his mama. No doubt, Brynne's life would've been totally different if her dad had lived. She still remembered getting excited when her dad would come home and running out to greet him. He'd taught her to ride a bike.

She tried hard to stay focused on what Sheriff Loughlin was saying without glancing toward the window. She'd worked hard to prove herself, and this morning after finding Reagan gave her hope that the other deputies might begin to believe. It was important that she earned the confidence of her team members, but especially the lieutenant.

"We don't have a description of the vehicle the man was driving, and that is a big step in learning our man's identity. If our victim regains consciousness, we might have our answers shortly, but we can't put our faith in that happening."

Brynne didn't believe that. They should have faith that Reagan will make a recovery.

"Let's get out there and catch this guy."

As soon as everyone started mingling, Brynne led Fergie toward the door.

"Taylor…" The sheriff's voice carried across the room. She stopped. "Yes?"

"Good job finding our victim."

"Thanks." Her gaze caught Dotson's. She hoped he wasn't disappointed Fergie had found Reagan instead of Jeff and Boss. Surely not. That would be childish of the lieutenant.

"I'd like for you to visit with the victim's mother. See if you can learn anything more. I'm hoping we can find out who was targeting the teen."

"Yes, sir." As she stepped out of the room, she felt several pairs of eyes on her. She went out the side door to the parking lot and made a beeline to Jace's truck, which sat just inside. "What are you doing?"

"Waiting for you." At her glare, he continued. "Okay, I'm

worried about you. And I want to help catch whoever hurt that teen."

"You're just a rancher." It was his turn to shoot her a warning glare. She held her hands up. "That came out wrong. You're not in law enforcement."

"True. That didn't stop me from finding you in a deep freeze." He smiled. "I was thinking it might help to talk with the mom and thought you might be of help."

She chose to ignore his rebuke. "I'm on my way to see her. Sheriff's orders."

He shrugged. "Guess I'll see you there."

"I don't want you messing this up for me." She sighed.

"How would I mess anything up? There's nothing to say I can't visit with the parent of a victim found on my land. That would be uncaring of me. You can ride with me," he said with a smile, the dimples making him heard to reject.

"No." She shook her head. "I have Fergie with me and her crate."

"Okay. I'll see you there."

Annoyance tugged at her. There was no need for them to take separate vehicles, and he probably knew she would cave. "You can ride with me."

Amusement danced in his eyes as he strode around the front of her truck to the passenger side. "Do you know which hospital she was transferred to?"

"Yeah. It's in north Dallas, about an hour-and-a-half drive." At his nod, she continued, "Don't you have any work to do?"

His eyes cut to her. "I always have work to do. You know that. But some things are more important. I have a couple of high-school boys I hired to help me on the ranch. They'll be there after school."

As she pulled out of the parking lot, she noticed Lieuten-

ant Dotson and Sheriff Loughlin coming out of the building. They looked her way, no doubt noticing Jace riding up
front with her.

Awkwardness filled the cab. It'd been forever since she
spent time with Jace. She stole a glance at him. A dark, short
beard lined his chiseled jaw, and his piercing eyes still captured a serious, but kind look. She wasn't even certain how
he pulled off the combination, but he did. He looked even
better than he did back then. He'd filled out and appeared
more like a man instead of the kid she remembered. The
worn and dusty Stetson didn't hurt either.

She swallowed. This might not have been a smart idea.
Maybe she should've told him to take his own vehicle.

"You look good, Brynne."

Evidently, he'd been looking at her, too. She kept her voice
even, removed her sheriff's department baseball cap and ran
her fingers through her hair. "Thanks. You like the way I'm
wearing my hair these days?"

He shook his head. "Being a canine handler suits you."

Her attempt at humor fell flat. She forced her eyes to remain on the road, lest he think his compliment meant too
much to her. It did, but he didn't need to know that. And he
hadn't taken the bait to mention how rough she looked in
the weather last night or today. "What makes you say that?"

"You were always good with animals. Remember when
you nursed that rabbit back to health after it was attacked
by a hawk? You ran screaming to scare the hunter away and
then brought the injured prey back to the barn."

She grinned. "I can't believe you remember that. I had
forgotten all about it. When Celine found the rabbit in a
shoebox in my room, she'd almost killed it with a broom,
mistaking it for a huge rat."

"I remember." He chuckled. "She made you keep it in the

barn after that. Then next day, it was gone. I would've figured you becoming a veterinarian or something. But helping people makes even more sense. You were a caring person. To animals…and to Tessa and Carrie."

It'd been forever since she'd thought about Tessa. Just nine at the time Carrie disappeared, Brynne hadn't had contact with Tessa since she was removed from the Mooney home. "Have you heard from Tessa? Did she continue living with the Mooneys?"

"You don't know?"

"Know what?" Why would Jace assume she knew what any of her foster siblings were doing? She'd been moved out to another family. More siblings. Different parents. The routine had grown old. She'd even forgotten a few of the kids' names she'd lived with over the years. How pathetic was that?

Jace stared at her. "She married Sam."

"Sam. Your brother?" At his nod, she felt her stomach tie in knots. Sam was six years younger than Jace, just two years younger than her. "How did that happen?"

He smiled. "Like it always does. Little brother went to medical school in Dallas to become a doctor. It took him six years to become a pediatrician. When he'd come back in, they'd go out. By the time he graduated, she was just beginning college."

Brynne tried to take this in. Her thoughts went back to Carrie and how she had to get ready to move out on her own, and how all of them had to leave the Mooney foster home after they turned eighteen if they stayed in the system. "How did Tessa make it on her own?"

"Scholarships. She moved into the dorm and worked on campus."

"I'm happy for her. What did she get a degree in?"

"Office management. She worked in Sam's medical practice until they had my nephew. Liam is four now and in preschool. Everyone has to keep an eye on him and Huck to keep them out of trouble. Reminds me of how Sam and I were growing up."

"That's wonderful." It seemed like everyone had moved on with their lives and started families. She was happy for Tessa. She truly was. Everything had worked out for her, which was rare in the foster system.

"She owes a lot of it to you," Jace said, watching her.

"Why? I didn't do anything."

"Yeah, you did. Tessa admired you. You need to go see her."

She marveled at Jace's words, but didn't quite believe them. He was trying to make her feel better about Carrie. She and Tessa and Carrie had shared a room for two years, but Tessa had only been nine when Brynne was moved out of the home. Surely, Tessa had been too young to have a lasting impression of Brynne. But just the thought of her helping the young girl did make Brynne feel better, especially after failing Carrie.

"I mean it. You and Tessa would get along. She's a caretaker. She watches Huck sometimes for me. Since Liam only goes to school half a day, she's always willing to give a helping hand when she can with Huck."

The rest of the ride to the hospital was mostly quiet, which was how Brynne preferred it. She thought of Tessa and Carrie. It was strange how things had worked for some, but not all. Maybe if Brynne found closure on Carrie's disappearance, she'd feel better about her own life, about her mission. It was strange to hear Jace say he saw her as a caretaker. She always felt like personal success was just out of reach.

She pulled into the parking lot and attached Fergie's leash to her harness. Her tail wagged happily as she jumped out of the truck. Jace secured his handgun in the console, and Brynne locked the vehicle. Brynne had called ahead to get permission for Fergie to enter the hospital. SAR dogs could visit with proper documentation and shot records. They walked into the trauma unit together. She dreaded this conversation. She could only imagine what Reagan's mom was going through.

Glass doors automatically opened, and they walked down the hall with Jace's boots softly clicking. Several people were seated in the waiting room, some of them scrolling on their cell phones, and others were watching the news on television. A middle-aged woman who had been at the search party sat in the corner nursing a cup of coffee. Her lips curled down on the corners of her mouth and lines streaked across her forehead.

"Mrs. Hepburn."

"Yes." She glanced up in question. Her gaze went from Brynne's uniform logo to Fergie and finally to Jace. "Have you caught the person who harmed my daughter?"

"No, ma'am. I'd like to ask you a couple of questions about Reagan if that's alright. More personal questions."

Her brow wrinkled. "Uh, certainly."

An older man with stark white hair got up from his chair and moved for the other side of the waiting room. "I'll sit over here to give you more room."

"Thank you." Brynne sat in the vacated chair and Fergie sat at her feet. Jace stood against the wall, but close enough that he could hear.

Dark circles sat under the woman's eyes. Her hands clutched her blouse, showing her stress. "I've already talked to the sheriff's department."

"Yes, I know." Brynne sat close so they wouldn't have to talk too loudly. "That was mainly to get a description and picture of Reagan. My name is Brynne Taylor. Do you know who may have targeted your daughter?"

She shook her head. "No one. Reagan is a sweet kid and well liked. She has no enemies that I know of. This is why I don't understand why she lied and took off to Hope Valley like she did. I trusted her."

The hurt in the woman's voice tugged at Brynne's heart-strings. But the big question was if Reagan was Carrie's daughter. She hated to ask, but she had no choice. Brynne pulled the woman's hand into her own. "This may sound like an odd question, but was Reagan adopted?"

Mrs. Hepburn's eyes grew large, and she pulled her hand away. "How did you know that?"

Brynne's chest tightened. Did she want Reagan to be Carrie's child? Jace's gaze collided with hers and questions danced there. She swallowed, trying to gain confidence. "I'm afraid Reagan may have been trying to find her birth mother. I assume this was a closed adoption, and you don't know who the mother is."

Intelligent green eyes stared back at her. "No, I don't know who the mother is. Or the dad. Would you like to tell me how you know this about my Reagan? We never told her."

Never told her she was adopted, or never told her how she became a ward of the state? Brynne squirmed in her chair. "Sixteen years ago, a friend of mine had a baby that she couldn't take care of. I dropped the infant off at the fire station."

Tears glistened in the woman's eyes. "You left baby Reagan at the fire station? Who's the mom? The dad?"

Brynne could feel Jace's eyes on her. "It's a long story, but Carrie Kaufman, the mom, was my foster sister and lived in the Mooney home where Reagan disappeared from."

Mrs. Hepburn's hand went to her chest. "Did Reagan meet her birth mom?"

"No, I'm certain she didn't." She shook her head. "Carrie disappeared sixteen years ago, only three days after she delivered Reagan."

"Her birth mother disappeared. What does that mean? Like she left her foster home?"

How did she answer this? Brynne drew a deep breath. "I don't believe so. There was someone at the foster home that shouldn't have been." Okay. She wasn't making sense, but Mrs. Hepburn searched her face.

The woman asked, "You believe someone hurt the mother?"

"Yes, after she delivered Reagan."

"But there was no evidence of foul play," Jace added quickly. "Carrie wasn't the type of person to run off."

Brynne stared at Jace. She'd never told him about the guy who locked her in the tack room. Now was not the most desirable way to tell him, but she prayed it would encourage Reagan's mom to help. "Actually, there was a man there the night Carrie disappeared. I'm afraid he might have hurt her, which is why I was concerned about Reagan."

She could feel Jace's eyes on her, but she kept her attention on Mrs. Hepburn.

The woman blinked before her eyes narrowed. "How could anyone give up that precious baby? What kind of human does that? There are adoption agencies throughout the country with couples lining up to adopt. But to discard a precious infant not knowing what will happen to her is unfathomable. What if a person with ill intent, or even an animal, had gotten to Reagan? She could've been hurt, or worse."

Because Brynne had stayed to watch to make certain one of the firefighters found her before Brynne left. Now was not the time to mention it. "I'm sorry, Mrs. Hepburn. I didn't mean to upset you."

"My daughter is in there fighting for her life because of something that happened years ago. No one thought that was important to mention until now. The sheriff should've told me. And you have the nerve to come here and question me about her. How dare you."

Everyone in the room had grown quiet and was listening to the conversation.

Jace stepped up. "We appreciate your time, Mrs. Hepburn." He turned to Brynne. "Ready to go?"

She climbed to her feet, her legs shaking. This hadn't gone as she expected. Or had it? She never should've helped Carrie give the baby away. Moisture blurred her vision as she gripped Fergie's leash and walked out of the waiting room.

Jace put his hand on the small of Brynne's back as they exited the waiting room. Carrie had a baby. He'd never known. He had thought she had put on a little weight. But even then, she hadn't looked big enough to have a baby. As soon as they were in the hallway, he whispered, "We have a lot of talking to do. But before we leave, let's see if one of the nurses or doctors can tell us anything."

Brynne shook her head. "Let's just go."

He took in her pale complexion. "Give me a second. You came here to gather all the information you could."

"You're right, of course."

Brynne's face had paled, and he could see the encounter had taken a toll. He had a lot of questions he intended to ask. They approached a double set of doors that led to the trauma unit. There was a buzzer with instructions, so Jace pushed the button.

A voice came over the intercom. "Yes?"

It wouldn't hurt to try. He said, "We'd like to see Reagan Hepburn."

"Visiting hours start again at five p.m."

"Is there any way we can get an update on her condition?"

"Are you a member of the family?"

"No, ma'am." He'd known the chances of getting in would be unlikely. "My friend is with the sheriff's department."

"I'm sorry. Family members only."

"Thanks, anyway." He turned to Brynne and shrugged. "Didn't hurt to try."

From behind them, a voice said, "What do you want to know?"

He looked over Brynne's shoulder to see Mrs. Hepburn. "We're trying to figure out who attacked your daughter. I was wondering if the nurses or doctor would know when Reagan can talk with us."

"It's okay." Brynne shook her head. "We're sorry to have bothered you."

The woman stepped closer. "You're not bothering me. I didn't mean to strike out at you. I'm just so upset. Reagan has never done anything like this before. It's strange to have a baby that you knew was dumped at a fire station with no name, no identity. Discarded like she was nothing. That was part of the reason we never told Reagan she was adopted. We didn't want her to let her beginnings create doubt of her self-worth."

Fergie stared curiously at Mrs. Hepburn. The woman glanced down at the dog and smiled. The Saint Bernard seemed to pick up the emotional situation.

"I understand," Jace said. A boy had been placed with the Mooneys who'd been left on the playground at a fast-food restaurant and his parents never came back. Jace knew the damage was real. "Have the doctors said when she may come to?"

She shook her head. "She's stable right now. There's fluid on the brain, but the doctor doesn't believe it is life-threatening. They are keeping her sedated for at least twenty-four hours. Maybe longer. They're waiting for the neurologist to run another test. I wish they would let her come around so she can tell me what happened. If someone harmed her on purpose, I want them caught."

It had only been several hours since she was found and at least her condition wasn't fatal. Jace had heard nothing but good about this hospital, so Reagan should be receiving the best medical care.

Mrs. Hepburn tilted her head to the side. "Tell me about the girl who went missing from the Mooney home after she gave birth."

Brynne glanced down at her hands. "It's believed Carrie was attacked. She was never seen or heard from again."

Mrs. Hepburn's hand covered her mouth, and she shook her head. "I think you're right. It sounds like she could be Reagan's mother."

"We don't know that for certain," Jace interjected. "But the sheriff's department is working on it. This is why Brynne thought it was important to talk with you."

The woman's gaze went back to Brynne. "I sincerely apologize for my attitude earlier. I've just been so worried. Do you have any ideas of who may have done this since the mom was your foster sister?"

"I don't. But we're doing everything we can to find out."

"Okay. Wait." Mrs. Hepburn dug through her purse and pulled out a receipt from a grocery store. She jotted numbers across the back. "Here's my number. Call me if you have any news or questions. I just want Reagan to come home and be like it was before."

Could the teen ever go back to how she was before? Probably not. Brynne reached into her back pocket and pulled out a business card. "If you think of anything that might help, please call."

"I will."

Silently, they walked out of the hospital to her truck. Brynne carried her shoulders stiffly, and her complexion was still pale. Once Fergie was loaded into her crate and they were on their way, he said, "Tell me about it."

"I don't want to talk."

"If Reagan is Carrie's child, then it's important, and you need to tell the sheriff. Does he know about the man who was there that night?"

"I know what I need to do," she snapped. "I'm not clueless."

"I never said you were." But he also wasn't going to let this drop. Carrie was the key to this case. "I was around Carrie all the time and had no idea she was carrying a child." When Brynne didn't respond, he said, "Do you know who the father is?"

"Don't you think I would say so if I did?"

"You're not being very helpful, so, no, I don't. You didn't think it was important to tell me about there was a man there the night she disappeared?" The glare he received was expected, but it wasn't only Reagan who was in danger, but Brynne. "You're not breaking your promise to Carrie if you tell."

Her head jerked around. "I don't know who it is. Don't you think Reagan's birth father is the first person I thought of? And if it was him who hurt Carrie and attacked Reagan, what kind of person does that? What else is he capable of?"

"Capable of threatening and hurting you. I'm on your side." He reached across the console, but she moved her hand to the steering wheel. "You really don't know who the father is?"

A few seconds ticked by before she whispered, "I don't."

He believed her. It was difficult since she didn't confide in him about Carrie's baby. He'd thought they'd been close. This was all he was going to get of her for now. If Carrie didn't tell Brynne about the baby's father, then the guy must be someone who could cause Carrie trouble. Or vice versa.

He tried to remember whom Carrie had dated back then. There were a couple of different guys. One was from high school, and one was someone she worked with. How did she have a baby and keep it a secret? Carrie had always had a curvy figure, and she disappeared at the beginning of December. She must've had the baby at the end of November. He'd been interested in Brynne and not Carrie, so he hadn't paid attention to how she dressed. She'd probably worn sweats or sweaters to hide her condition, but what did he know?

The traffic thinned out and the four-lane highway stretched out in front of them. He glanced at Brynne. Were there other things she'd kept from him? He'd always believed they were close. "Do you want to talk to me about that night? You know the details you're not telling. You can start with the man you saw and why you didn't tell Sonny and Celine or the police."

She half sighed and half growled, like she was frustrated. "He threatened if I told anyone about seeing him, he'd not only hurt me, but Tessa."

He shook his head in disbelief. "How could you have kept that from me? I would've—"

"Would've what? Gone to the police? And then Tessa, and maybe me, would've disappeared like Carrie? Tessa was only nine at the time. Just a kid."

His head swam with the information. He didn't know if he was more scared for Brynne's safety or hurt that she hadn't confided in him. "We'll never know what I would've done, because you kept it a secret, but I would've been there for you."

"Sure, you would. Just like you promised we would stay in contact with each other no matter what happened between us. It took you two years to reach out." The words were tossed like a dagger.

She made her point. He decided against delving into their relationship right now because she would use it as a diversion. "Are you going to tell me what happened that night besides the man threatening you? Do you know what happened to Carrie? Did you see more than what you're saying?"

"I had gone to bed early that night. If you remember the Mooney's van broke down while they were away at Ricky's basketball game."

"I remember." Ricky was Brynne's older foster brother.

"Like I said, I'd gone to bed and sometime later heard Carrie's car. I didn't realize she hadn't come into the house until I heard a scream. I went to check it out and saw a light on in the barn. When I got there, I saw blood on the floor and then a man dragged me into the tack room, threatened me not to tell and hit me over the head. I woke up to find the room locked. Sonny let me out when they got home."

"Did you tell Sonny what happened?"

She shook her head and shrugged. "Not really. After they got home and found our room empty, they began to look for us. Mr. Mooney went inside the barn to check things out when he saw the door open. He found me locked in the tack room. I told him I didn't know how the tack room got locked, but I'm certain he didn't buy that story. I also told Celine I didn't know where Carrie was. I was sent to bed but heard them up talking for a long time. They made several phone calls to friends to ask if anyone had seen Carrie. The next morning, they called the sheriff's department."

Jace remembered waking up to his parents talking about Carrie missing. The news spread fast, and he had immediately gone to see Brynne. She'd claimed she went to bed the night before and didn't know where her sister was. They could go over the details more later, but right now they needed to make a plan. "What are we going to do now?"

She didn't look at him. "I'm not certain. I've been thinking it over."

"And…"

This time she glanced toward him. "It makes me wonder if someone other than the biological father knows Reagan is his child."

"Why would you question that? You mean like the guy's wife or girlfriend?"

"Could be. I want to avoid zooming in on one suspect. No tunnel vision."

"I hear you, and I can help you. I was never in law enforcement, but I was in security."

"I only need help from the deputies."

"Brynne, I worry about you. I can afford to take a few days off and let the ranch hands run everything. I don't mind. Did the man say anything to you before he locked you in the freezer?"

She sighed.

He could tell he must have. "Are you going to answer me?"

"He told me I shouldn't have come back."

"You're incredible. Then it was the same guy you saw years ago the night Carrie disappeared?"

"Probably. There's nothing to worry about."

"You're in over your head, Brynne. Don't be stubborn. If you won't accept my help, talk to Sheriff Loughlin. Whoever this guy is, he is no one to play around with."

"I'm very aware of the danger," she snapped.

Bam. A vehicle hit them, causing his head to hit the passenger window. Jace looked over the seat and saw a black Escalade right on their tailgate.

Brynne floored it. "Check on Fergie."

He leaned over the seat and looked in the crate. He would've opened the door, but he didn't want the dog to get flung out in case Brynne's truck was hit again. The Saint Bernard stood in her crate and looked at him.

"Down, Fergie," Brynne said. The dog obeyed.

The SUV hit them again, and this time her vehicle lurched toward the ditch. She let her foot off the accelerator and gained control. She hit the button on her radio. When the dispatcher answered, she said, "Need assistance on Highway Ninety-nine, just outside of Stone Falls. Black Cadillac Escalade has rammed me twice, but I can only get a read on the first two numbers on the license plate. JH."

"You're out of our county, but I'll alert Elk County Highway Patrol."

After she hung up, she slowed and pulled into the ditch.

"What are you doing?" Jace yelled.

"If he's hoping to run me off the road, I'm not going to give him a chance." She removed her gun from her holster. "There are too many innocent civilians on the road."

As the Escalade raced by, she got off a shot at the vehicle. The back panel window exploded, and the driver pulled to the shoulder and did a U-turn. "Here he comes again. You need to get out of here," Jace said.

"Hang on."

He closed his eyes for a split second. Maybe sitting still was a better decision. The truck lurched into gear and took off. As their speed climbed fast toward the Escalade, he retrieved his gun from the console.

Instead of ramming them, the SUV pulled over and then

whipped around behind them. Jace checked the rearview mirror. "He's coming this way again."

Brynne didn't say a word, but Jace had to wonder why the guy didn't hit them head-on. A rental moving van traveled slowly in front of them, and Brynne went around the van about the time the black vehicle drew closer. "Watch out."

The SUV got right on her bumper and hit the driver's-side bumper, spinning her out. "Hold on," she yelled.

The maneuver made her truck spin left, out of control and into the median. When they came to a halt, she asked, "Are you okay?"

"Yeah—go, go, go." He pointed as the Escalade came back at a running start.

Lights swirled and sirens blasted. Jace looked over his shoulder to see two patrol cruisers headed their way from the opposite direction. The SUV peeled out, with grass and mud kicking up behind it.

She hit the gas again, but this time, her truck barely moved. She slammed her hand on the steering wheel. "Great."

No doubt she'd have to rock the truck back and forth to get it unstuck, but he decided not to state the obvious. As one of the officers pulled on the shoulder of the highway close to them and stopped, he let her understand his position. "This is getting out of hand, Brynne. Next time we may not come out uninjured."

SIX

Brynne's neck ached from her head being snapped back. She was annoyed Jace was right about her needing help. But most of all, she was scared. Being a search-and-rescue K-9 handler, most of the danger she'd been in had come from the weather, like an avalanche or being in a serious situation, as in going down steep grades to find someone who'd disappeared. Like the time a child had wandered off from his tent while his family had been camping in the woods. He and three other boys were playing hide-and-seek in the woods when he got lost. Fergie had found him over five miles from where he was last seen, and a mountain lion was in the area. She had used her bear spray to scare the cat away.

But this was different. This guy wanted her dead and kept returning. Several law-enforcement officers she'd worked with had been targeted by criminals, but no one in SAR.

After she gave her report to the officers from Elk County, a BOLO—be on the lookout—was issued on the Escalade.

She and Jace had been quiet on the ride. Her hand still quivered from her nerves being on edge from the near-death experience. The man was getting bolder, not caring who was around. And the fact that Jace was with her told her he didn't care who was hurt.

Jace said, "Will you at least not fight me on it?"

He didn't have to specify what he meant. "Maybe."

His right eyebrow arched. "This is no time for stubbornness."

"Yes, Jace. I know. If I could only figure out why someone wants to hurt me."

"Either you know something that this guy fears, or someone doesn't like me." At her look, he chuckled before sobering. "This has to do with Carrie and Reagan. So why does he lump you in with them? Unless someone wants revenge for a case you worked." He looked at her curiously.

She shook her head. "I don't think so." But she'd been thinking so much about Carrie and Reagan, it made her wonder about his question. She pulled into the lot of the department, where Jace's pickup was parked. "He must believe I can identify him from the night of Carrie's disappearance."

"Can you?"

She shook her head. "Not really. I didn't see his face. It's just…"

"What?"

"Peaches." At his questioning look, she said, "I smelled peaches that night."

"Okay. That's a weird thing to recall."

"I know. I'm not even certain I didn't imagine it." She shrugged. "But later I was sure I had smelled it on his breath."

"Come by the ranch."

She wanted to say no and go home to research the case, but could she work if she had to look out the windows and keep watch for the shooter? "Okay. For a little bit, but I need to go talk with the sheriff first."

"No better time like the present." He pointed to the sheriff's truck. "I'll wait for you."

"Keep an eye on Fergie for me. Would you?"

"You know I don't mind. But I'm going to let her out of her crate so we can visit."

"Okay." She waited until the Saint Bernard stood and draped her head over the seat while Jace petted her, whispering something she couldn't decipher.

Dread filled her as she walked into the department to talk with Sheriff Loughlin. He had been a good boss, and she couldn't keep any details of the case from him. Her boots quietly clicked on the commercial tile floor as she walked through the lobby. Allison glanced up at her as she passed the dispatcher's desk.

"You okay, Brynne?"

She nodded. "Shook up a little, but no injuries. I need to speak with Loughlin."

Allison gave her a sympathetic smile. "He's in his office."

"Thanks." She paused just a moment at the sheriff's door with her hand on the knob and drew a deep breath. She needed to get this over with. Needed him to know what was going on so he could help solve the case. She couldn't put herself or her team in danger because they didn't have all the facts. Hopefully, he would understand. She knocked and opened the door.

The sheriff glanced up. "Come on in, Brynne." He indicated the chair across from his desk. "Have a seat."

She took the plastic chair and darted a glance into his dark, knowing eyes. She had the feeling she couldn't hide anything from him even if she tried. He had a weathered, intelligent look about him. She tried not to squirm. "There's some things I need to tell you about this case."

"I thought so. I'm listening."

Against her will, she twisted in her seat. "More than just about the attack yesterday and today. I'm afraid this goes back sixteen years ago."

"You need to be honest with me, Brynne. We're a team here at Rockford County. We work together."

"I realize that, sir. I don't know where to start." There was so much to say.

The lawman leaned back in his leather chair. "Why don't you start with your visit with Mrs. Hepburn?"

"Reagan was adopted, just as I suspected." She spit the words out too fast.

His expression was unreadable, and he waited for her to continue.

"If you'll remember when you hired me, I told you I was from the area. Or at least I had been from that area for a short period of time and had lived with Sonny and Celine Mooney. In their foster home."

"I remember."

Her mouth went dry, making swallowing impossible. "You may have heard of a girl named Carrie Kaufman that disappeared sixteen years ago. She was my foster sister."

"I remember the Kaufman girl. Foul play was not suspected, if I recall."

She glanced up at the ceiling and prayed for courage. "That's not exactly true." She went on to tell him about the night Carrie disappeared three days after delivering a baby, about the blood on the floor, and the threat Brynne had received from the man.

His eyebrows drew in. "That was quite a burden on a young girl."

"Yes, sir, it was. I believe Reagan is Carrie's daughter. And I'm even more certain now that I have visited with the teen's mom."

The sheriff drummed his fingers on the desk. "You believe this case is connected?" He thought for a second. "That would mean the man is also after you."

"Yes, I believe that is true. I should've talked with you earlier, but I had no idea I would be thrown into a freezer or that the man would be at the Mooney place last night. I didn't want to show up this morning and not be on my best game when I met with the search party. I thought it'd be better if I went out there alone since I hadn't been on the property since I'd been moved."

His gaze narrowed. "You should've talked with me, or the lieutenant."

"I realize that now. I had no idea I would be attacked. I think the suspect would have to be Reagan's biological father."

"But you said Carrie did not tell you who the father was."

"Correct."

The sheriff stared at her for several seconds, as if he was mulling the situation over. "I'll have Sergeant Lancaster look into the possibilities of who the father is. We should be able to get permission from Reagan's mom to get her DNA. Hopefully, we learn who the father is in a few days."

Dennis Lancaster was an older, competent investigator who'd been with the department for over thirty years. "That's what I was thinking also. I remember a couple of guys Carrie had been seeing at the time. If only she would have confided in me."

"Is there a reason you think she kept his identity a secret?"

"I don't know. I always thought we were close, but it has always bugged me. Maybe we were not as close as I thought."

"Brynne, you're a good officer and a very good K-9 partner with Fergie. But we're a team in the department. You need to trust us to do our job. And trust us to take care of you."

She knew what he said made sense. But somehow, she constantly feared being dropped again by someone she trusted. Mayva, the captain in charge of the K-9 unit in Denver, had been tough on all the handlers, resulting in the department having a high turnover rate. If Brynne told the sheriff why she was hesitant to put faith in others, his reservations about her would be confirmed. "I realize that, sir."

"Leave your list with me and our investigator will look at others also. Besides boyfriends, do you know anyone else who might hurt Carrie? Or Reagan?"

"No." She'd asked herself the same thing, but she kept returning to Carrie's baby.

"Okay. I don't want to be so laser-focused that we overlook other potential suspects. We're running names of people who own a black Escalade with letters JH in the license plate. Forensics will be trying to match up tire impressions when we get our list. We'll stay in constant communication with Mrs. Hepburn and with the doctors at the hospital to see when Reagan is able have visitors."

"Do you mind if I check out some of the boyfriends if I let Sergeant Lancaster know?"

He scratched his forehead as he thought. "I'll need to know if you visit with any of the suspects and where you are. Whatever you learn, I need to be kept apprised."

"I understand. Thank you." As she exited his office, she almost bumped into Lieutenant Dotson. "Oh, excuse me."

"Everything okay, Taylor?" His head tilted to the side as surveyed her.

"Yeah." She didn't wait around for him to ask anything more. She felt his eyes on her as she walked away. Had he been eavesdropping?

She couldn't help but feel like she was skating on thin ice. The sheriff had said they were a team, but was it true? Or would a few critical words from Dotson have them looking for someone to replace her?

SEVEN

A minute later, Brynne waved a hand at Jace, who was standing by her truck. It sounded like he'd been talking to Fergie. "I'm here. Thanks for keeping an eye on her."

"No problem." He gave her a thumbs-up and handed her Fergie's leash before heading for his own vehicle.

She put Fergie in and climbed into her truck. She glanced into her rearview mirror. "Did Jace keep a close watch on you?"

Fergie gave a slight whimper and laid her head on her paws.

Brynne couldn't help but laugh. "Don't go getting too attached to the cowboy."

But as soon as the words were out of her mouth, sadness descended on her. When this was over, maybe she and Jace could be friends—even if they were distant friends.

She pulled onto the road. Only Jace seemed to be following her, but she'd keep an eye out just in case. Twenty minutes later, she slowed as she passed the Mooney place. No vehicles were in sight. The barn door was closed. The yard was marked with tire tracks from this morning's search. Once past her old home, she turned into Jace's drive. As she drove down the long driveway, she was amazed at the number of improvements that had been made. Had Jace done this or had his dad?

After a long dreary day, the sun came out and sat low on the horizon, creating a majestic sunset over the ranch—like a beautiful picture. The older farmhouse sported a new coat of white paint and was trimmed in cedar. A large stone fireplace stood at the front, along with a walkway. The home looked more appealing than the light green color it had previously been painted. There wasn't much landscaping—no flowers—but the place had a rustic appeal. Much of the fencing had been replaced, and the barn had a new tin roof. Cows grazed in the pasture, and a couple of horses were in the pen by the barn.

As she pulled around back, she noticed a toy dump truck half-buried in a sandbox and a tractor-shaped swing dangling from the pecan tree in the backyard. The thought of Jace being a dad still amazed her.

When she got out of her truck, she said, "The place looks much the same as I remember it, but better. You've made a lot of improvements."

He nodded and casually replied, "Thanks."

But she thought her compliment meant a lot to him. Or maybe she was considering how she would feel if he said the same for her home.

"You want to see Flash?"

"Flash? Not the same horse I used to ride. He must be thirty years old."

"The same. But he's only twenty-five and healthy."

"That's still old for a horse. I'd love to see him again." She had taken to the horse almost immediately when she moved to the Mooney ranch. The first time she met Jace was when she went to meet Flash for the first time. Sonny Mooney had hollered upstairs to tell them if they wanted to ride, their neighbor had brought a horse over. Carrie had no desire to see the animal, but Brynne and Ricky had sprinted down the stairs and out the front door. When she jumped off the porch, the first thing she saw was the tall black horse with the white mark on his forehead that was in the squiggly shape of a lightning bolt. Then a tall, lanky teenager wearing a Western shirt with sleeves cut out and a beat-up cowboy hat stepped in front of the horse, dragging the reins behind him. Jace's tan was deep, and his friendly smile won her over at first sight.

As silly as it was, she still remembered his first words to her. *Mornin'. I'm your neighbor. Name is Jace. I heard Sonny and Celine had a new daughter and thought you might want to meet Flash.*

He had called her their daughter. Not a foster kid. Not an orphan. Even though it was rare for a child in foster care to be an orphan, it didn't stop people from calling them that. And he had introduced himself by name. It had been a small gesture, but one that always stuck with her. To this day, people would refer to her as the Mooney's foster child.

She had a name and had been happy to share it with her rugged neighbor.

"Okay. Let me get Huck and give Mom a break. He loves to see the horses. Uh…" He shoved his hat back on his head. "My boy is scared of big dogs. Last time he was around one, the dog accidentally knocked him down."

"Fergie is great with kids, but I'll make certain she's extra gentle." The promise was more to reassure Jace, for the Saint Bernard was always calm. She let her partner out of the truck while she waited for Jace to return. Her nerves were a tad on edge. Surely, that wasn't because she was about to meet Huck, but probably because it had been almost two decades since she had been to Jace's ranch. Now, it didn't belong to his parents, but to the man himself.

A moment later, Jace came outside with a dark-haired boy

at his feet. The cute little guy wore boots and denim overalls. When she approached with Fergie, Huck's eyes grew large.

"A dog! Hold me." The boy clawed at his dad's jeans and held his hands in the air.

Jace scooped him. "It's alright. The dog is nice."

"This is my Saint Bernard, Fergie." Brynne smiled and held the leash snug. Fergie's ears went up, and she cocked her head to the side, staring up at Huck with a soft gaze. Her tongue lolled and her whole body wiggled with the movement of her tail. As if sensing Huck's hesitation as he still clung to Jace's neck, Fergie sat but continued staring up.

Jace said, "Fergie's nice. She likes kids."

Huck continued to cautiously watch the dog. "Hold me."

"I've got you. We're going to show Brynne the horses before it gets dark."

"Okay." The boy's gaze barely went to her before returning to Fergie.

Jace shot Brynne a sympathetic smile.

She whispered, "It's okay. A lot of kids are scared of bigger dogs."

"I wished you could've seen him with Buddy, our older collie. The two were inseparable. But he died last year at the age of fourteen."

Huck didn't take his eyes off Fergie. Her heart swelled at the sweetness. She'd always had a soft spot for kids.

Even with everything going on over the last day, being with Jace reminded her that there were good things in the world. She couldn't believe he still had Flash. When she stepped around the barn, her eyes landed on her most favorite horse of all. His coat wasn't as shiny, and he had white hair around his mouth, but he still looked great to her. "Does he still ride?"

"No one gets on him much anymore, but he'd love to sometime."

She plucked some stray hay from the ground and threw her arm over the top rail of the fence, holding out it out. Flash hurried over and nibbled from her hand.

Huck looked at Fergie before he squirmed in Jace's arms, telling him he wanted to get down. His dad put him on the ground.

Brynne made certain Fergie was out of the boy's reach, and continued feeding the horse.

Huck followed her cue by grabbing hay and holding it out to the big black. "Here, Flash."

She glanced at Jace. "Will Fergie make Flash nervous?"

"Nah, he's used to dogs."

"Be gentle, Fergie." She dangled the leash at her side, giving her a little more room. The Saint Bernard climbed under the wooden fence and sniffed. The horse bent down, seemingly curious, but quickly lost interest.

Brynne again held out straw, and the horse put his head over the fence. She wrapped her arm around him and laid her head against his as she rubbed his neck.

The horse sat still for several moments as she rubbed his neck, and then he nodded his head up and down.

"He remembers you."

"No way. It's been too many years."

Fergie barked and stared at Brynne.

Both she and Jace busted out laughing. He said, "I think she's a little jealous."

"I think you're right." She smiled as she snapped her fingers at her friend. "Come here, Fergie. I'll give you attention."

Fergie trotted over, and Brynne leaned over the fence to pet her.

Huck kept a leery watch on the dog while he held hay out for Flash, and the horse quickly took it from him.

Jace moved a boot to the bottom rung of the fence. "He mostly keeps to himself nowadays. Believe what you will, but he remembers you."

She still wasn't certain that was true, but it made her feel good, either way. Flash been young and energetic back then.

"I remember when my dad brought him home." Jace stood beside her, his elbow touching hers. "The big guy was anxious and wouldn't get near anyone, but you wouldn't leave his side."

The warmth of his touch cut through her long-sleeved shirt. "I was determined."

Jace chuckled. "You wouldn't go home. My mom was worried about you."

"I didn't know that."

"The first three nights you fell asleep outside his stall in the hay. My dad told my mom, and she insisted he take you home. Mom was afraid you'd get hurt by a horse, or some kind of animal, like a skunk or a possum would scare you good."

Brynne shrugged with a smile. "I knew if I spent time with him, I could gain his trust."

"It worked. And Dad let Sonny and Celine know where you were at so they wouldn't worry."

"I loved the lightning mark on his forehead and his demeanor. Your dad and Sonny started referring to him as my horse, and I can't tell you what that meant to me."

"I knew."

She looked at Jace, but he continued watching Huck and the animals. He probably did know how much little things meant to her. But if that was true, why didn't he call her and come see her after she moved? She'd texted him her new address on her first night in Amarillo after she was moved from here.

When Fergie crossed back under the fence, Huck held his hands to Jace again. She wished the boy would give her dog a chance, but sometimes it took a long time for people to overcome their fears.

After they fed Flash, they moved down to the other pen, where a big Appaloosa and an older chestnut were watching them with their heads held high, evidently waiting to be fed.

The colorful spotted coat pattern of the Appaloosa was beautiful. She pointed. "That horse is stunning, too."

"Doo is a feisty guy and enjoys working the cattle."

"Doo?" she repeated. "What kind of name is that?"

He shrugged. "It's short for Dapple Doo. My granddad used to have a horse called Shorty and another one called Blackie."

"Doo sounds like a type of shampoo." She giggled. "I suppose you were being more creative than they were."

"Most ranchers I know don't spend a lot of time on that sort of thing. I was thinking outside of the box. But for your information, the name means inquisitive personality. It fits him."

"It really does. He's handsome."

"Don't let him hear you say that. I'll never be able to get work out of him again."

It felt nice talking and joking with Jace. He'd always been able to get her to lighten up and enjoy the small things.

After they fed the other two horses, Jace asked her if she'd like to come inside. Being that Huck was afraid of Fergie, Brynne didn't want to bring the dog into the house, but also didn't want to leave her outside. At the back door she asked, "Do you have a room I can leave her, so she doesn't frighten your son?"

"Sure. I'm sorry about that, but I appreciate it. Buddy had a dog bed and a couple of toys Fergie can use." As she stepped inside the dining room with Fergie, Jace hurried through another door that looked like it was going to a garage.

Huck stood on the other side of the room and watched them warily. When Jace returned, carrying a plush bed, the boy's eyes lit up.

Brynne smiled. "Fergie is going to use Buddy's bed. Okay?"

Huck frowned but nodded his head.

"Thank you. She appreciates this. Do you have a utility room?"

"I do, but it's cluttered with laundry. She can stay in the dining room."

She led the dog into the corner of the spacious room and Jace put the bed on the wooden floor.

He turned to the Saint Bernard and swept his hand over the bed. "It's all yours."

Fergie sniffed the bed and turned a full circle before lying down. She grabbed the purple dragon toy and began to chew.

When Brynne looked up, she noticed Huck standing around the corner of the kitchen cabinet with his attention on the dog.

"Stay," she called more for Huck's benefit than Fergie's.

Just like the outside of the home, the inside had a different look. It was more rustic and looked to have been freshly painted. "I like what you've done to the place."

"I work on it when I have time, mainly during the winter. A project or two every year. It's not easy to find the time tending to Huck and helping my mom."

"Come on," Huck said with a wave of his hand.

"Son, Brynne doesn't have time for that."

She smiled. "I don't mind, Jace. Really." She followed the little guy to the back of the house to a bedroom that contained a bed in the shape of a covered wagon and *Huck* spelled out in wooden letters on the wall. Toys littered the floor and more lined the shelves. "I love your room."

"Watch." He grabbed a truck and yanked on it until it transformed into a robot. He held it out to her so she could see.

"That is such a cool toy."

"Yeah." He smiled, then dropped the truck/robot, grabbed a small, soft football and threw it to her.

Even though the move took her off guard, she caught it. "You have a good arm."

The boy nodded with enthusiasm. "Yeah."

"That's enough, Huck." Jace stood in the doorway. "I need to talk with Brynne."

She'd been having a good time relaxing for the first time in the last two days. But Jace was right. There was someone out there that wanted her dead. Now was not the time to let down her guard.

EIGHT

Disappointment clouded the boy's expression and his shoulders slumped, but he was not to be deterred. He picked up a plastic horse. "This is Flash."

She couldn't help but laugh. The horse was close to Flash's color and the boy was so eager to show off his things it tickled her. She rubbed her hand through his hair. "He does look like Flash. He's probably fast, too."

"He is." Huck's eyes lit up. He waved the toy through the air like it was running.

Jace smiled and shook his head. "Okay, I'm going to talk with Brynne now." When they stepped out of the room, he mouthed, *Sorry.*

"I don't mind at all. He's a sweetheart, Jace."

When they entered the kitchen, he said, "Thanks. Sometimes I worry about being at work and him spending time with both Tessa and my mom, the odd family arrangement will have a negative effect. But he seems to thrive."

"Are you kidding me?" She couldn't believe he'd say such a thing. "He has multiple people in his life who love him. That can't be a bad thing."

He searched her expression. "I suppose you're right. Now, who do you think is after you?"

His abrupt change of subject was a snap back into reality.

This wasn't a social call. "I don't know. If I did, I'd be check-ing them out right now. I assume it's Reagan's dad. Maybe the Mooneys know something."

"But you said they didn't know she was even pregnant."

"I know, but maybe they can help us figure it out. Car-rie and I were close, but I also had things going on in my life." Like spending all of her free time with Jace. Had there been warning signs Brynne had missed because she'd be distracted? Possibly.

Jace shrugged. "It wouldn't hurt to talk to them. But it's getting late. You can stay the night here, and we can drive over there in the morning."

She didn't want to cast doubt on everyone she used to know, but this was important. "Yeah. I'd like to visit with them. It can't hurt. But Fergie and I can go home. You think Huck and your mom will be okay here?"

"I'll be fine."

Brynne spun around to see Grace Jackson standing in the doorway dressed in a pair of jeans and a soft beige sweat-shirt that said *Howdy* across the front. Her salt-and-pepper hair was cut in wispy layers and came to her shoulders. Even dressed in jeans and in her socked feet, she still came across as classy, like she could've been in a gourmet coffee commer-cial lounging on a soft sofa with colorful pillows and a fire in the background. "Mrs. Jackson, it's so good to see you."

She waved her hand. "Please. Call me Grace. I agree with Jace, dear. I think it'd be safer if you stayed here with us. I'm sorry to hear about the teen. I've been praying for her recovery and for all of your safety." She turned to Jace. "Go talk to Sonny and Celine in the morning if you think it will help. You know I don't mind watching Huck. For now, I'm going to whip something up for supper."

"Thanks, Mom."

"It was nice seeing you again, Mrs., uh, Grace." Brynne understood why they would want her to stay here, but she hated to lean on them. Once she did, she would be brought right back in the middle of this family, making it harder to pull away when the assailant was caught.

As Grace began to dig through the pantry, Brynne pulled Jace to the living room. She kept her voice to a whisper and said, "I appreciate the offer, but I need to go home."

Jace folded his arms across his chest while he waited for Brynne to finish explaining why she needed to leave. "Are you through now?"

"I just don't think it's a good idea that I get used to depending on you. Or anyone else," she added.

She couldn't fool him. She wanted the help, but she was too stubborn, sticking to her rules to do what was best. "Feel free to leave if you want. We need to get an early start in the morning. If you're attacked on the way home or once you get there, it'll throw all of our plans out the door. There is not one benefit to you putting yourself in danger. I'm not asking you to become a part of our lives." He saw the hurt cross her face and instantly added, "I'm just trying to be practical. Your dog is here, and I know you carry extra food in your truck. Huck is safer with me here, but you're making it where I must worry about you being alone at your house. I can't divide my time between Pepper Creek and the ranch. Tessa and Sam should be here in the morning to help Mom. You can sleep in the third bedroom. I have security cameras. This place is as safe as you can get."

Her chin lifted, and she stood tall. Which meant she was a tad angry. He didn't mind, as long as she was safe and made the right decision. He cared for her and did not want her to get hurt. Another thing was he wanted to explain why he hadn't kept his end of the bargain about continuing their relationship after she'd moved.

She stared off at the corner as Huck ran into the room.

Huck asked, "Will you eat with us?"

Bless his son for the interruption.

Brynne kneeled down beside him and smiled. "I would love to, Huck." She looked back to Jace. "Don't think this changes anything."

He decided not to gloat that he'd gotten his way. A few minutes later, his mom showed Brynne to the third bedroom. It wasn't used often, except if Tessa needed to separate Liam from Huck during naps. There was a twin bed in the corner for that occasional time when they had extra guests. While Brynne and his mom were in the room, he heard them talking, and his mom was giving Brynne some extra clothes that Tessa kept there.

He stepped out into his garage and called Sam. After he gave his brother an update, he asked, "What are your plans tomorrow?"

"It's Thursday, so I need to go to work. I have two important appointments. The others can be rescheduled to next week if I must. What do you need me to do?"

"Brynne and I were planning to visit Sonny and Celine. I hate to leave Mom here alone with Huck. Do you think Tessa would want to help?"

"I know she would." Sam spoke to someone in the background and then came back to the phone. "Would you like for us to come stay with y'all tonight? I can leave from there in the morning."

Jace thought about it. Even though he hated for them to go to so much trouble, it would make him feel better to have extra backup. He was not used to having dangers hitting at every turn. He also believed if Tessa was here, Brynne would be more content.

"That would be helpful, brother."

"You've got it. Give us a while to get our things together."

After Jace got off the phone with Sam, he felt a little better about the situation. He walked back into the kitchen and asked his mom to set the table for three more people. He could still hear Brynne playing with Huck. His mind went back to Maggie. She had said she wanted kids and to live on a ranch. So many dreams that matched up with his. But when it came down to it, she was dissatisfied. Even Huck hadn't kept her content.

He walked to the doorway and watched Brynne, unnoticed. She was reading a book to Huck about a dog who had traveled to the moon for cheese. As she read, she exaggerated her words and her facial expressions. Huck was so engrossed in the story, he didn't notice his daddy was even standing there. He didn't know what to make of the instant connection between her and his son. Brynne was distrustful of others, and he didn't blame her. Part of the reason for her skepticism was his delay in reaching out to her.

"What are you doing?" Brynne smiled like she was amused.

He shrugged. "Thank you."

Her eyebrows squished together like she didn't understand. Then she looked at Huck, seeming to conclude it was for reading him a story.

Thirty minutes later, Sam and Tessa showed up. Liam ran in the door to play with Huck but suddenly he stopped and turned around. "Hey, a dog."

Fergie had been lying in the corner watching people come and go. Brynne had taken her out earlier to feed her and for a break in the yard. Liam hurried over to her side.

Sam sternly said, "Wait. What have we told you about approaching dogs you don't know?"

Liam looked down at his feet. "To ask first."

"That's right." Sam turned around and found Brynne. "Is it okay for Liam to pet your dog?"

"It's alright. And her name is Fergie."

Liam kneeled down and petted Fergie on the head. "Hello, Fergie." After a second, he turned around. "She's soft. Can she come play with us?"

"I'd rather her stay on the bed until Huck gets used to her." She turned around. "Huck, would you like to come pet her?"

Huck stood at the far side of the room and watched. "No."

Jace took the opportunity again to show Huck that he could trust the dog. He reached around Liam and rubbed Fergie under her jaw. "She's such a nice dog."

When Tessa came through the door, her eyes lit on Brynne and they both hugged. Tessa said, "It's so good to see you."

"You, too."

Jace stood up. It always amused him how women who hadn't seen each other in years could pick back up like no time had passed. They talked so fast, he wasn't even sure what they were saying. But he was glad to see Brynne enjoy yourself now that she'd been brought together with the people she used to know. With a possible killer targeting her, he couldn't claim it to be happy reunion, but at least she had support.

Throughout supper everyone talked and laughed and stayed on enjoyable topics. Nothing heavy or serious. Jace had gotten up twice to walk around the house and check outside and the security cameras, and to make sure no one had approached. Sam was the only one who seemed to notice. When Jace returned to the table for dessert, his eyes connected with Sam's, and an understanding passed between them to stay observant.

Tessa had just finished telling a story about Sam playing hide-and-seek with Liam. "Sometimes Sam likes to jump out and scare him."

Brynne's expression brightened. "My dad used to do that with me. I had to be about five. He would go outside and tell me to count to thirty. Since I couldn't count that high, Mom would tell me when to go look. I'd run outside calling his name. He was a great climber and would often hide in the cedar trees. He would call my name—'Brynne-Brynne'—repeatedly, until I found him. I remember one time he hid in the back of his pickup bed. He jumped up and scared me half to death. That was too funny." Everyone laughed and no one seemed awkward, but Jace could feel the change in the air. Brynne rarely talked about her dad or mom. The fact she could relax to talk about good times was great. But no one said it. As if she understood, she glanced around the table and then back down into her plate. "Sorry." She shrugged. "I just thought of it."

His mom said, "Don't you dare apologize. I love hearing family stories."

Brynne shared another story, and by the end, they were all laughing.

Jace quietly ate the last bit of peach cobbler, and he got back to his feet to check the perimeter one more time. It was completely dark outside, and the side yard was only lit by the security light. He hadn't seen anyone or anything suspicious, but he didn't trust their safety enough to get some sleep.

Sam came up beside him. "We'll take turns standing guard tonight."

"It's a deal."

After he made certain there were plenty of pillows, clean

sheets in the bedrooms and toiletries in bathrooms, he went to get his son dressed for bed. When he came into the kitchen, he could see Brynne in the living room with Fergie. Standing beside the big Saint Bernard were Huck and Liam, who were both combing her fur.

"Look, Dad. She's nice." Huck beamed up at him. Even though he still stood a little back, he had made great improvements.

"I see that. I'm sure she loves being brushed by you boys." Both kids nodded.

"It's time for bed." Jace hated to ruin their fun, but he had a long night ahead of him. "Liam has school in the morning."

"Do I have to?" his nephew whined. "I can stay here and help with Fergie."

Tessa walked into the room with wet hair—apparently, she'd just showered—and clapped her hands once. "Sorry, but Uncle Jace is right. It's time for bed."

"Can I sleep with Liam?" Huck asked.

Jace's mom came into the room. "I'll be glad to put them to bed. But it's up to your parents if you can sleep in the same room."

Tessa shrugged. "I don't mind."

The boys yelled for joy.

Huck ran up to Jace and gave him a hug, and then he turned to Brynne and held his hands up. She gave him a squeeze, and then both boys ran out of the room behind their grandmother.

"Thank you for being so patient with Huck." Jace leaned against the doorframe. "Fergie won him over."

"I knew she would if given the time." She plopped down on the couch. "I'm exhausted."

He stared at her for a moment, not certain what to say.

"Sam and I will keep watch. I don't know if you can, but try to get sleep."

"I appreciate it, but I called Sheriff Loughlin after your mom showed me to my room, and he is making certain a deputy drives by every hour or two."

Her dark hair spilled over her shoulders. He understood wearing it back it in a ponytail while working, but he preferred it down, as it was now.

She curled her feet beside her on the couch and eased her head back. "I pray we learn something tomorrow from Sonny and Celine."

"Me, too. Speaking of prayers, I need to go say them with Huck." He started to walk away but stopped. Again, he couldn't help but compare how much better she'd been with his son than Maggie. His wife had acted like she couldn't wait to get away from their son.

Brynne stared at him like she was waiting for him to say something.

It was in him to tell her how much it meant to him of how good she was to his son, but he thought better of it. She'd already admitted she had no intention of keeping their relationship going after this case was closed. "Good night, Brynne."

NINE

Brynne loaded Fergie into her warm truck as Jace said goodbye to his son. They were already running much later than she had planned. After Liam left with his dad to be dropped off at preschool, Huck seemed disappointed. She figured Jace was also leaving instructions for his mom and Tessa, should they have any trouble while they were gone. The air had a cold bite today, and the forecast was calling for a chance of snow.

"Your dog could've stayed there." Jace slammed the passenger door and rubbed his hands together to shake the chill.

"I know. But I like to keep her with me when I can. I'm still on duty. Do you think they'll be fine here?"

"Yeah. Mom and Tessa will both be here until one of them picks up Liam from school. Sam will be home shortly after that. I'm hoping we'll be back before then."

They drove off and pulled onto the country road. "I agree. And you really didn't have to ride with me. We could've taken two vehicles."

He didn't respond. She knew he was determined to stay near her, no matter what she said. It took twenty minutes to get to town and most of their conversation consisted of chitchat. Brynne didn't mind because it kept her mind off the danger they were in and who from her past wanted her dead. Carrie had gone missing many years ago, and now Reagan, presumably Carrie's daughter, was fighting for her life. What was it about the Mooney foster home that had put them all in danger?

Thinking about it gave her a headache and filled her with dread.

She pulled into the drive of a quaint brick home that was surrounded with colorful petunias. A large sign, decorated with pictures of a sunflower and bumblebees, had *Welcome* printed on it. A calico cat was curled under a blanket in a white wicker chair on the front porch. The feline's ears twitched when they got out. Brynne left Fergie in the truck in case they had dogs inside the home that didn't take to other animals.

As Jace pushed the doorbell, she noticed the scripture that hung above the door. *Hebrews 13:2. Be not forgetful to entertain strangers: for thereby some have entertained angels unawares.* That's what the couple had been to her. She'd been a stranger and they had taken her in. Even though this house was obviously smaller than the one in the country, it still held the Mooney philosophy of a home that proclaimed everyone was welcome.

The door opened to a tall, hunchbacked man with white hair. Brynne barely recognized him. His gaze went from Jace to her, and his eyes lit up.

"Brynne Taylor. Is that you?"

She nodded and smiled.

He opened his arms wide. "Welcome home."

The words seemed so wrong given the moment. She'd come here wondering if they knew something about the danger that seemed connected to them, but he was as friendly as he had been when she was younger. She stepped into his outstretched arms, returning his hug.

"Celine, honey, you'll never guess who's here." He waved his hand. "Come on in. Celine will be glad to see you."

A framed folded American flag hung above the archway. Some of the same photos that had been in the Victorian home hung on these walls. The painted picture of a tractor. The black-and-white photo of Celine's side of the family in front of the family-owned general store in the town of Bunker Springs that no longer existed. Joy and sadness brought on by the passage of time made Brynne's throat clog.

They stepped into the living room, and Sonny spoke louder. "Brynne Taylor is here."

Gnarled, arthritic hands and thin hair sat upon the older woman. "What's that?"

He spoke even louder. "Brynne Taylor is here."

The woman looked at her then. "Come hug my neck, darling."

Brynne gave her shoulders a gentle squeeze. She guessed that the Mooneys had been in their mid-fifties when she'd moved in, but they had seemed so full of life at the time. They must be in their late seventies now. They'd changed a lot more than she'd expected.

Sonny looked at both of them. "What can I do for you?"

Jace said, "We'd like to ask you a few questions about Carrie Kaufman and some of the kids who lived in your home."

"Come on in and have a seat," Celine said. She indicated a new sofa.

Sonny didn't sit, but stood in front of the fireplace. Brynne shoved up her sleeves. She could hear the central heat running and found the home too warm for her comfort.

"We've gone over the girl's disappearance a thousand times if that's what you're asking about. I have no idea where to find her," Sonny said.

Brynne was happy to let Jace ask the questions. The frailness of Celine took her by surprise. Even though Sonny had gray hair and slumped some, he still looked heathy.

Jace cleared his throat. "Did you know Carrie had a baby before she disappeared?"

"What? No. What are you talking about?" Her foster dad's face went red. "The girl never had a baby."

Brynne wondered about his reaction. Of course, if he had no idea, the thought would be a shock. But still. He almost seemed angered.

"What about Celine?" Jace continued. Sonny's reaction did not seem to deter the cowboy. He looked at the older woman. "Sometimes women have more of an instinct with that kind of thing."

"Let's not bother her." Sonny made the comment like his wife wasn't in the room.

"What's that? Is he asking about Carrie?" Celine said loudly.

Brynne put her hand on her back. "Carrie had a baby right before she disappeared. Were you aware of that?"

The woman's gaze connected with hers. Even though the woman seemed to be struggling, Brynne could see she understood exactly what she'd said. She opened her mouth to answer, but Sonny cut her off.

"None of the girls in our house ever had a baby, except Julie, but she was with child when she was placed with us. Then she was moved to a group home that specialized in helping teen moms care for themselves and their children."

Brynne had heard of such homes after she was out of the system. Maybe Julie had come to live there after Brynne had moved out, because she didn't recognize the name.

Jace looked at Brynne as if asking her to take over. He was right—she would be better at explaining. "A teen girl went missing from your old home the last couple of days. Her abandoned car was found on your property."

"Yeah. We know. The sheriff called us to get permission to search our place. Was she found?"

"She was. But she had been attacked and was injured. There's more. Someone shot at me. I didn't get a good look at the man, but someone is trying to kill us."

Celine stared at her for several moments. "I'm so sorry. That's terrible. What does this have to do with Carrie?"

"We believe the missing teen is Carrie's child, the one she gave up."

"Oh, my." Wrinkles of concern crossed the woman's forehead. "That poor girl."

Whether she had referred to Carrie or the daughter, Brynne didn't know.

Jace said, "We were hoping you could help us figure out who might want to hurt Reagan—the teen—and Brynne."

Sonny's brow wrinkled.

"Honey." She looked at her husband. "Do you think…"

He shook his head as if telling her to be quiet. "I have no idea who might want to hurt you. But it's no one from our home."

That wasn't what they'd asked. "I never thought it was," Brynne said quickly. "I know Carrie had a baby because I was with her. Do you know who the dad might be?"

"No, we don't," Sonny huffed and folded his arms across his chest. "Carrie had several boyfriends, and I'm still not certain she had a child. Maybe it was someone else's."

"I was with her," Brynne repeated. "I dropped the baby girl off at Hope Valley fire station. There's no question about it." Brynne knew this must be a surprise to them, but she didn't like they didn't believe her.

Jace glanced her way. "Would you let us know if you think

of anyone? The attacker is a man, but that's all we know. Maybe if you think about it…"

"Come back sometime." The older man moved for the front door saying their conversation was over. "We'd love to visit."

A hand clamped down on Jace's shoulder as Brynne stepped out on the porch. He turned to see Sonny looking at him oddly with his eyes squinted. "I'd like a minute."

"Uh." Jace glanced over his shoulder to see Brynne continue down the sidewalk. "What is it?"

"You need to get that girl to back away from this case," Sonny said. Firmness danced in the man's eyes, along with the warning.

"She's not going to do that. She works with the sheriff's department. It's her job. What's this all about?"

"If I remember correctly, you always cared about the girl. I even believed you two might become a couple someday. I see the way you looked at her back then, and still do. If you care, get her away. Let another deputy investigate."

Jace didn't appreciate the threatening tone. "What's really going on, Sonny? What aren't you telling me?"

The man looked him straight on. "All I can say is there are bigger things at play here. If you want to keep her safe, she needs to quit asking questions before she stirs up a hornet's nest. She needs to back off."

"Brynne would never walk away from helping Reagan or anyone else. She's determined to find out what happened to Carrie."

Sonny sighed. "I care about her, too. Brynne was like a daughter to me and the missus. I don't want her to get hurt."

"I will protect her."

His voice dropped. "You don't know what you're dealing with."

"Then enlighten me. Like you said, Brynne is important to you."

"I can't." Sonny shook his head. "I'm trying to help. If you care about her at all, tell her to let someone else work this case. Remove herself."

Jace searched his expression but shook his head. "I can't do that."

"Don't say I didn't warn you."

As Jace headed away from the home, he noted Brynne inside of the vehicle watching him. Warn her about what? Sonny's comment made no sense, but a feeling of doom settled on his shoulders. There was no way Brynne would back away even if he asked her to. She'd been close to Carrie.

As soon as he got into the vehicle, she asked, "What was that all about?"

"Sonny wants you to back away from the case."

"No way."

He thought that would be her reaction. He didn't blame her.

After a minute, she asked him thoughtfully, "Did he say why?"

"Not really. He said if I wanted to keep you safe, I needed to convince you to let another deputy work the case. That you were stirring up a hornet's nest. He was adamant."

Her head jerked around, and her eyes narrowed. "That makes no sense unless he knows something he's not telling us. Did you notice how angry he got when I mentioned Carrie had a baby?"

"What are you thinking?"

She shrugged. "I'm not certain. Either he knew about it, or he was surprised by it. Sonny and Celine took pride in being good parents. Could be something as silly as it was irritating that they didn't realize what was going on in her life. Like they should've known, and it reflects on their parenting skills."

"Could be." His neighbors had tried hard to be good parents to children who carried a lot of baggage. They had raised three of their biological children and then decided to become foster parents after their youngest graduated high school. But they took the difficult cases, the older children that not many foster parents wanted to take in. Any teen could be difficult, but ones that had neglect or abuse in their background, or ones who were moved from home to home, like Brynne, were more of a challenge. He had to respect the couple for the love they had shown.

Several minutes ticked by without Brynne talking while she drove, and he felt the need to know what she was thinking. "It's been a long time since you've seen them, Brynne. I'm sure Celine's declining health surprised you. But I've been around them. The last few years have been tough on them. Sonny seems to do alright, but Celine suffered from a stroke two years ago and has heart failure."

"I had no idea. Silly, but I picture them just like they were sixteen years ago. But that's only part of it." She sighed. "They were the closest thing I had to a real family. They know more than what they were saying. It scares me. What if the people I thought were honest and good turn out to have skeletons in their closet? It's like there's no one good in the world. They were both encouraging to me, and now you tell me he doesn't want me on Carrie's case. They should know how important it is to me."

"There's plenty of good people, but we all have problems."

She turned to him with a sort of glare. "What about you? Do you have skeletons? Are you hiding something?"

The first thing that jumped to his mind was how Brynne was the one who had hidden something, that she had helped Carrie hide a baby and never told anyone. She'd dropped off the helpless infant at a fire station. She didn't know what would happen to the child or what kind of family might adopt her. But he kept his thoughts to himself. It wasn't her child to care for, and it would only manage to make their already strained relationship even worse. Then guilt tugged at him as he thought of how he hadn't contacted Brynne after she'd let him know she'd been moved to Amarillo. He hadn't told her how it had been Sonny who'd convinced him not to stay in touch. Looked like both of them had secrets. "I have no skeletons."

The look in her eyes says she wanted to believe him. "I hope not."

He didn't like where the conversation had taken them. "Anyway, I don't why Sonny wants you off of the case, but I felt I needed to let you know." He glanced at her, but she didn't respond. He half hoped she would let the other deputies investigate. The other half respected her if she stayed on.

He noticed the Juicy Burger on the corner and pointed. "This is the last place to get something to eat."

"I'm not that hungry, but I suppose you're right since I didn't eat breakfast."

"Me either." They both ordered a burger and fries and ate in silence in her truck.

When Brynne pulled into his drive and around to the back of his house, the first thing he noticed was the back door hanging on the hinges.

Brynne gasped. "Oh, no, what happened?"

Jace couldn't answer her right now as a knot formed in his stomach. She slammed the gearshift into Park, and he ran up to the house through the open door. "Tessa? Mom?"

But there was no answer. He continued through the house to his son's bedroom. "Huck?"

A moan came from the closet, and he threw open the door. Tessa was lying in a mound with her hair covering her face. He squatted on his haunches and pushed back her hair, exposing a big bruise across her forehead.

Green eyes stared up at him. She sobbed. "I'm so sorry. I couldn't stop them."

"Where's Huck?" He managed not to choke on the words.

"They took him." Her shoulders hunched and tears glistened in her eyes. "Go check on your mom. I don't know where she is."

Brynne said from behind, "I'll find her."

Jace's throat went dry, and he licked his lips. "Who took him?"

"I don't know. There were two men who surprised us when they broke through the back door. Both were wearing masks." Tessa tried to struggle to her feet, and Jace helped her to stand.

"Did you see which way they went?"

She stumbled into him, and he steadied her. "No. I tried to hide with Huck in the closet, but they found us. I didn't have time to get out of the house. After one of them hit me on the head, I heard what sounded like an ATV or motorcycle."

"Not a truck? Are you certain?"

"I can't be sure since I didn't see it, but it sounded just like Sam's ATV. I'm so sorry, Jace." Her gaze went over his shoulder. "Are you okay, Grace?"

Jace turned to see his mom and Brynne standing outside the doorway.

"I'm fine. Jace, I grabbed one of your guns but one of the men knocked it from my grip before I could get it cocked."

"I shouldn't have left Huck for you two to watch." When

he turned to Brynne, her eyebrows had drawn together in concern. But he couldn't take the sympathy right now. He had to find his son. "Come on."

Brynne followed on his heels. "We must call this in. We need help."

"I am going to find my son." He turned to Tessa. "Call Sam to stay with you."

"He should be on his way here with Liam right now." Tessa's face softened. "Be careful."

Brynne rushed up to his side before he walked out the back door. She said, "I would like for you to wait for me. We can't leave them alone like this. Fergie can help find Huck. I need something with his scent on it."

"Check his room. You can come with me or not. I will not wait another minute."

"Let me get my backpack."

He listened as Brynne told Tessa, "I'll call the sheriff's department and let them know what's going on. Do I need to wait with you? Or do you need an ambulance?"

"No." She gave Brynne a push.

Grace said, "The gun will not leave my side, and I'll stand guard. I was putting away laundry when I should've been paying attention. I will not make that mistake again."

Tessa said, "I'll keep a gun with me while I wait."

Jace hurried out the door and strode to the barn. He quickly threw a saddle on Doo.

Footsteps sounded behind him. "Fergie and I are going to help you."

He knew she was just trying to help, but he couldn't afford the distraction. "I don't want you to get hurt, and I can't watch out for you."

"That's not your decision to make."

He took in the determination in her gaze and knew it was

useless to try to talk sense in her. "What about the dog? Are you putting Fergie on my horse?"

"Of course not, but I'm sure she could. Glad to see you haven't lost your sense of humor," she added sarcastically. "I'll take your ranch Jeep and follow you where I can. I'll get out and walk if the two men got away on foot."

"Suit yourself. But be careful. I don't want to worry about you with two dangerous men on the loose. My main concern is Huck."

"I'm a deputy."

"Keys are under the seat." He watched as she nodded and then took off with Fergie for the Jeep that sat under the shed. He prayed she didn't get hurt.

He thought about when he lost Maggie. She'd been at work...or so he thought. Instead, she'd been having an affair with a resident doctor at a lake house his family owned. Maggie had left the home at six in the morning. The fog had been thick, and she'd lost control of her car on a sharp curve. Her vehicle flipped several times before slamming into a tree. He remembered getting the news and being so confused about why his wife had been thirty miles away from the hospital where she worked. At first, he was naive enough to believe that the sheriff's department had identified the wrong victim.

Evidently, Jace wasn't good at keeping track of his family. If he didn't rescue his boy, he'd never forgive himself.

TEN

Brynne called the sheriff to let him know what was going on. He promised to send a couple of deputies out to Jace's ranch.

She followed behind Jace's horse. They were moving out at a gallop, but she was still able to see the ATV's tracks in the grass. She put the Jeep into low gear and tried to avoid mud holes. Fergie sat behind her. Her heart went out to Jace for the fear and guilt he must be feeling. She couldn't help but believe this whole situation was her fault. Jace was just trying to help her. It was time to catch these guys. Why did all this have to happen? What did it have to do with Carrie and Reagan?

It had to be the father of Reagan that was behind the attacks.

Tessa had said there were two men. Had there been two men all along?

Was Huck being used as bait to get them away from the house? If so, it had worked.

The path became more cluttered with small bushes, but the other night's rain had mostly dried up. The Appaloosa ran at a good pace. The kidnappers must have had about a thirty-minute lead on them. It would be easy for them to get off their ATV and load it onto a trailer, and be out of the county by now. She prayed that was not the case.

Occasionally, she lost the ATV tracks, but then they would pick up again. She studied Jace's back as she followed closely and noticed the tightness of his muscles. It would be dark soon, and the temperatures would be dropping. She prayed they would find Huck before then.

Jace rode into a ravine and when he came out on the other side, he turned back to glance at her. She shrugged her shoulders, telling him that she wasn't certain whether to try to cross or not. Being that this was a four-wheel drive, she decided to take her chances. If she got stuck and had to get out and walk out the ravine, what difference would it make? Either way, she would wind up on foot. She backed up a few feet and then floored it. The ground was bumpier than she thought, and the Jeep pitched and went straight down to the bottom. A trickle of water ran through the base, but she kept the accelerator down.

The big tires spun, slinging muck everywhere. Fergie got down in the back. Brynne continued to floor it while turning the steering wheel. The vehicle went sideways before it started to gain traction. It pitched as it climbed up the other side. As she exited the ravine, Jace stared at her. He shook his head and kept going.

If she thought that was the worst of the path, she was wrong. Two sets of ravines, although smaller, spidered across in front of her and an enormous wash sat in the middle. There was no way she could cross that. The ATV sat about fifty yards away in the trees, telling her the men were on foot.

Again, the feeling that they were walking into a trap came over her. The men wanted them to pursue them.

The Appaloosa waited on her. She was going to have to get out of the Jeep and let it sit where it was. Taking Fergie's leash, she got her out of the vehicle and went around the wash as best as she could. Jace turned around just as her feet sank into the mud.

She waved him on to keep going, since she did not want him to waste any time while Huck was being taken farther away. But Jace stopped, anyway. She really wished he would move on, but at the same time appreciated the gesture.

"You can go on," she hollered. "I have Huck's shirt, and we'll follow the path the guys took."

"Are you certain?" Concern etched his brow. "I don't want to leave you behind. I don't know where these guys are."

"Please. Keep going. I will stay on the trail but if you can find him quicker, then please do. Time is of the essence." Never had a cliché been truer.

"Okay. I can still see their tracks, and I must be gaining on them. I really appreciate this, Brynne."

She watched him as the horse weaved through the trees and soon disappeared. Her heart hurt for him, as he must be scared to death of losing his boy. She trekked through water, her boots disappearing into the muck. Coldness seeped throughout her being. She was wearing her long-sleeved sheriff's department shirt, but it did little to keep her warm. Gray clouds filled the sky. She didn't know the temperature, but it looked like snow in the near future.

When she reached the ATV, she opened the small storage box on the bike and was surprised to find it unlocked. There was nothing inside except for a broken fishing lure and a screwdriver. Nothing that would give her an indication of the identity of the two men or what their plans were. It's not like she thought there'd be a map marked with a red X.

Fergie's paws were covered in mud, but she plodded on a couple of feet in front of her. It helped her to have Fergie with her, not only to help find the boy, but also for the companionship. Occasionally she heard the crashing of limbs and once the horse neighed.

Shadows grew, and darkness fell fast. A raindrop hit her cheek. Or was that sleet? It was so light, it was difficult to tell. It still bothered her that the men took Huck into the trees instead of getting far away. It had to be some kind of trap to bring them to the boy's rescue. As much as she realized this was the case, there was no choice but to go after him.

She could no longer see the prints left by the horse's hooves, but Fergie kept leading the way.

Her radio came to life and Lieutenant Dotson's voice sounded. "We're here at Jackson's ranch."

"Fergie and I are on the trail. Jace is ahead of me on horse-back. The ATV has been abandoned and the suspects must be on foot. It's extra muddy."

"We're headed your way. Keep your GPS on and be careful."

Silence descended on the dark woods, and she paused to listen. She heard nothing except the soft patter of raindrops and kept going at a slower pace. Suddenly a gunshot echoed through the trees.

Her gun was at her side. She took off at a run, and Fergie was still ahead of her but she reined her in a little closer.

The Appaloosa sprinted by her headed back toward the barn, kicking up his feet, and disappeared from sight.

Jace!

As she drew nearer to the place Jace had gone, she slowed to a walk, keeping alert. Where was the shooter? Then there was the sound of footsteps, slowly moving through the woods. But it was a strange sound, like the gait was strained.

A silhouette moved against the trunk of a tree, and she paused, keeping Fergie's leash tight. She aimed her gun.

"Brynne." The gasp of Jace's voice sent chills down her spine.

She hurried toward him. "Are you alright? Were you hit?"

"I took a bullet to my thigh." He gritted his teeth. "They're close. And I lost my gun. I need to find it."

"Did you see Huck?"

"I only saw the flash from the gun. I didn't see anyone. But I'm certain if Huck was close, he would have hollered for me. They must be keeping him at a distance. I think they were waiting for us."

Her heart constricted. "Lieutenant Dotson and a couple of deputies are here. Wait for them, and someone to take you back to the house."

"No way. I've got to save my son."

"Don't be stubborn. You will only slow us down and you don't have a weapon. Let me go find Huck for you."

Jace shook his head. "Let's go."

"You'll only slow me down." She understood, or at least understood as much as possible as someone without a child, but Fergie would find the boy. "Give us a try."

"This is not a contest. Kidnappers have my son. I'm going. You can go ahead of me if you wish, but I'm not going back."

His words stung. She was not trying to outdo him in finding Huck. She stared at him for a moment, conflicted. If the men were armed, and she had to assume they were, it would be more dangerous to separate. Jace was compromised. But he wasn't going to listen, and the truth was it'd be better if Huck was found now. "I'm going ahead. But, Jace, be careful. No doubt this was a trap to get us in the middle of nowhere and attack. Huck is the bait."

His gaze narrowed. "I realize that."

Pain radiated through Jace's leg as he watched Brynne take off through the brush. He shoved the throbbing to the back of his mind. When he got to the area he'd taken the bullet, he hunted for his gun. The undergrowth was thick with many vines and rough brush. For several minutes, he searched under plants, and even got down on his knees to get a better look. The pain was unbearable, and he barely made it back to his feet.

He took off again. If he came upon the men, he hoped he could outwit them to get Huck back. There was no way he could return to the ranch for another weapon. After a few steps, his foot came down on a limb, sending pain shooting throughout his entire body. The direction Brynne had gone was almost impassable, so he swung out to the right, where the path was less cluttered. He picked his way through carefully, trying to avoid the thorns and briars that plagued the area.

For a few minutes, he could hear the faint sounds of Brynne and Fergie's movements. Moisture ran down to his knee from the bleeding wound. He would need to get medical care, but he could do that once Huck was back in his arms.

As he came to the edge of the clearing, a rustle came from the right. He paused to listen. More rustling about thirty yards in front of him, to the left. Being that there were at least two men, Huck, Brynne and Fergie, he couldn't be sure who was where. He waited for several moments, but there was only silence.

Stepping as lightly as his thigh would allow, he picked his way through, careful not to land on twigs or make noise. It was a difficult endeavor considering the shooting pain. One small step at a time, he made his way to the sound on the right. Every two or three steps he would pause just long enough to listen. It was possible the noise he heard was a rabbit or squirrel, but he wanted to check it out.

A small whisper rose in the cold air and then more rustling.

He strained to make it out, but could not decipher the words. He took another step forward and leaned against a small pine tree for support. Again, there was swishing, like something moving. But there were no more words.

A flash of white moved to his right. It was so quick he wasn't certain he'd imagined it. He took a step in the same direction, moving through the brush, careful not to make a sound. Without a gun, it could be a death wish.

As the tree coverage grew denser, his view darkened. He needed to make certain he did not come upon one of the kidnappers. Continuing slowly, he moved closer to where he saw the white color. An oak tree stood five feet away, and he crossed to it. Using it for cover, he eased his head to the side of it. He didn't see anyone, but movement sounded to his left. There was no way to know who was making which noise.

"Where did he go?" a man's voice whispered.

Jace swallowed hard. The man had to be talking about Huck. Hopefully, the flash of white he'd seen was Fergie.

Footsteps moved in front of him.

Brynne stepped into the clearing to his left.

The shadow of a man moved in front of him and took aim at her.

Jace's chest constricted as he leaped into motion. He landed beside the man and hit him like a defensive end on a quarterback, knocking him to the ground. Quickly, Jace rolled away and climbed to his feet. He darted between the trees as bullets sprayed all around him.

He didn't know if Brynne had been hit or had taken cover, but he kept going, hoping the man didn't follow. Several quick shots blasted, urging him to keep going. Suddenly, someone moved in his peripheral vision, and he came to a halt.

Brynne stepped up beside him, out of breath. "Have you seen Fergie or Huck?"

"I saw something white earlier. It was probably her."

"I got off several shots but don't know if I hit anyone. Come on." She motioned for him to follow.

A cry carried through the trees. Huck! When he came through the brush, his son was standing with his arms around the Saint Bernard. Jace scooped his boy into his arms.

Thank You, Lord.

"Good job, Fergie," Brynne said.

Twigs snapped behind them, and he and Brynne exchanged glances before continuing into the brush.

It was all he could do not to stop and just hold his son. He continued to give his gratitude to God for finding his son.

A man's voice yelled through the trees, but Jace didn't stop. Quietly, he worked his way through the undergrowth. There was movement and a few mumbles of voices from the man, but he could not tell from where they came from. He continued in a westerly direction as he whispered soothing words of comfort to his boy. "I've got you. You're okay." He gave him a kiss on top of his head. "Daddy's got you now."

They slowed to cross a shallow creek. Jace asked, "Where are the men?"

"I don't know. I fired at the one but don't know where the other one is." She ran her hand through Huck's hair. "It's so good to see him."

"We have to find our way out of here." He glanced around to get his bearings. "If we head back to the ranch, I'm afraid they'll be waiting for us."

"There's a storm brewing. We need to find shelter. Lieutenant Dotson arrived at your house, but is headed our way. We just need to take cover until the storm is over or the men are caught."

"My weather app called for a chance of thundersnow. But there's not a good place out here to hide." Huck only had on a pair of brown overalls with a long-sleeved T-shirt since he had been in the house when taken. His little checks were red, and his hands were freezing. Jace wrapped his coat around him as much as he could.

She looked at him. "Aren't we close to that abandoned town? What was the name?"

"You're right. Uh, Bunker Springs?"

"Yeah, that's it." Footsteps sounded in the trees behind them, moving quickly. She whispered, "Let's go."

Bunker Springs. It had been years since he had thought of that place. There were several old structures that had fallen into bad decay. Maybe three or four buildings that sat in a heavily wooded area, and he had no idea if any of them were still standing. He prayed for their sake, so they could find some place to hide until the other deputies either found them or captured the suspects.

As darkness grew and light flakes of snow floated to the ground, he worried about what would happen if they didn't find shelter soon. It was obvious these men had lured them into the woods by taking Huck. The only reason Jace could think of for the men to do that was an easy place to kill them and get rid of their bodies.

ELEVEN

Fergie led the way through the woods as they continued away from the two men. Brynne had taken a shot at one man in the clearing, but he had a mask on, which let her know it wasn't Jace she'd shot at. Brynne loved the country, but she'd had enough of it the last two days. A rumble sounded from the west and the wind picked up a bit. Thundersnow was uncommon, but it looked like the storm was headed their way.

The snow mixed with sleet and the cold began to seep through her gloves. She stopped long enough to get her Gore-Tex jacket out of her backpack.

They moved hurriedly through the brush. Considering Jace was injured, he managed not to slow them down. Now that he had Huck back, they needed to find shelter. Temptation to circle back in hopes of finding her team tugged at her, but she was fearful that was what the men hoped for. She'd only been to the abandoned buildings of the town once, and that had been close to twenty years ago. Would she be able to remember its location? There wasn't much time, so she hoped so. With every step, the snow picked up.

From somewhere in the distance, the engine of what sounded like an ATV hummed. Were the men leaving? Or hurrying to get in front of them?

She and Jace exchanged glances but didn't say anything.

"Come on, Fergie." Her heart rate sped up as she picked up the pace. Thorns tugged at her jeans and limbs slapped her face. She tried to keep an eye on her path, so she didn't fall or twist her ankle, but there was no time to slow down.

The woods grew quieter with only the sounds of the wind and their movement. Was the engine still running? She didn't slow but didn't hear it anymore. Hopefully, that meant the men had gone the other way, and not that they were again on foot pursuing them.

Or maybe they had separated.

As she came to a small clearing, she tried to determine which way to go, but this area didn't look familiar. There was no time to consider it. She went right where the brush was thicker, hoping the men would take the easier path. As soon as vines created a thick wall, she realized her mistake. She attempted to backtrack quickly but a crashing in the woods sounded behind her. At least one man was coming.

Her radio cracked with static. Lieutenant Dotson's voice came over. "We…don't. You—"

She attempted to keep her volume down. "I can't make out your words. We are headed west, southwest. Keeping to the woods."

Jace looked at her.

"I doubt he could hear me…"

"Can you text them?"

"I can try." She pulled out her cell phone. There were no bars showing, but she sent the lieutenant a message, anyway.

There was no choice but to keep going. Bending low, she pushed her way through a small opening and then stepped over a bush. She waited for Jace and Huck to make it over before she let the branches go. Again, she went down, this time to her knees, and crawled until she was on the other side to see another wall. Determined, she kept moving. If they intended to follow, they'd have to go through the same maze.

A huge rotting log was lying in front of her, and it collapsed as she went over it, catching her foot. She jumped in place on her left foot until her boot was released. Fergie stayed beside her, and snow collected on her fur. Brynne undid her leash so she wouldn't have to drag it behind her. Quietly, she patted her leg to let her know to follow.

Once she made it through the brush, more greeted her. Frustration bit at her for picking this route. Something glittered on the ground through the fast-falling snow. It was a piece of glass. It could've been from an ancient soda bottle that a hunter had discarded, but she prayed it was from one of the homes that had once been in the area.

Small, wispy branches stood in front of her, and she pushed her arm into them as hard as she could and forced herself through. A thin trail lined the ground, but it must have been one used by rabbits and smaller animals.

After another twenty feet of skin-tearing thorns, the foliage thinned to where she could weave through. She could no longer hear pursuit behind them, but it was possible they'd gone around the brush and would be waiting for them.

A rusty can sat on the ground, and what looked to be a rotted piece of lumber. Through the trees, a structure took shape. When she got to it, she realized it was an old tool shed or shop that was leaning and barely standing.

"I think we found it." Hope rose within her. She continued moving even though her arms stung from scratches. Fergie looked at her, waiting for a command. "Come, girl."

And then, another building that had toppled over and lay on the ground. All that was showing was the roof. Beside it was a rusty piece of antique farm equipment that Brynne didn't know what it was, but she remembered it from the last time she and Jace had been here. Finally.

The church would be to the left.

Jace said, "Up ahead."

Lightning lit up the sky and dark clouds swirled. A gust of wind hit them, blowing the snow sideways.

A stirring sounded behind them. She listened, hoping it was the trees rustling. But then a curse carried in the wind.

A buzz whispered for a mere second, making her wonder if the ATV had found a way around the woods.

They had gained on them. She hurried toward the trees and she could see glass reflecting. Small trees and dead vines almost covered the old church building, but Brynne could make out its form.

Large flakes filled the air, covering the ground just as thunder rolled. With Fergie at her side, she hurried through the opening where the door used to be just as a big gust of wind caused the building to creak. Jace limped right behind her.

There were a number of old wooden benches that had fallen into a variety of states of disrepair—from standing, some lying smashed on the ground. "Come, Fergie."

"You're not going where I think you are?"

"You know I am. It's the only place to hide." She didn't look at him as she hurried behind the pulpit. Wood and rubble covered the floor, and she dropped to her knees and started swiping the debris away, looking for a handle. A second later, her hand hit something solid. She stood and pulled up the wooden door.

A concrete baptistry lay in the middle of the pulpit. Two steep steps led to the bottom. "Come, Fergie."

The dog followed her into the square box and then Jace hobbled inside. An inch or so of partially frozen water covered the bottom, along with leaves, dirt and no telling what else in the muck. Her foot stepped on what felt like a stick.

Steps sounded from outside.

Fergie sniffed the floor of baptistry and then sat. She let out a sharp bark.

"It's okay, girl," Brynne whispered. She tried not to think about what they were standing in as she lowered the lid, engulfing them in total darkness. The dank air made her want to gag. She rubbed her hand across Fergie's fur to keep her calm. "Shh, baby. Quiet."

Jace followed suit as he stroked Huck on his back. "It's important to be real quiet, sport. Do you understand?"

Huck's lip puckered as he nodded.

Brynne leaned over. "I have my headlamp in my backpack if you need it."

"I think we're good," he whispered back.

Slivers of light illuminated through the slats of the trapdoor as lightning struck close, making her flinch. She shivered. Seconds ticked by, making her wonder if the men had missed the building. It wasn't easy to see with all the trees. Most of the windows were busted out, and even a couple of saplings had managed to spring up through the floor.

"Are you doing okay?" she whispered to Jace.

"Hurts something terrible, but I'll make it."

If the men found them, they would have no way of escape. She found her headlamp in her bag and clicked on long enough to withdraw her gun from the holster and check the clip.

"How many bullets do you have?"

"Three."

Jace groaned. "That's not enough. Let me have the gun."

"No way. You're injured, and I'm law enforcement."

She thought she heard him mumble the words *I know.*

Fergie whimpered again as she sniffed their surroundings. Brynne whispered for her to be quiet.

"In here." A man's voice sounded from outside, followed by footsteps. Thunder continued to roll in the background, making it difficult to hear the movements of the men.

Jace again put his finger to his lips to make certain Huck remained silent.

She positioned her back against the wall and held the gun straight up. She'd have to hit the first man on the first shot. That would leave two shots for the other guy, but he'd be more ready.

"Be careful," Jace whispered and then glanced at the boy.

She understood. This was dangerous for all of them, but it would be extra scary for Huck.

"Do you see them?" the man with a deep voice said. She wasn't certain, but the voice sounded familiar, like he was the one who attacked her.

"No. There are footprints outside so they must be close. Check the add-on restroom."

She didn't recognize the first voice, but the second one sounded like the man who'd thrown her in the freezer.

All of them seemed to hold their breath. If a person never looked inside this old building or one like it, then they might not know there was a baptistry in the pulpit floor.

Minutes passed and then more.

Fergie rested her chin on Brynne's knee. She gave the dog's head a rub with her free hand, but kept the gun trained, pointing up.

The danger seemed to have passed but there was no guarantee the men wouldn't be back. If Jace wasn't hurt, they could run for it. They'd just have to wait until the deputies arrived. A check to her phone showed that her text had not gone through.

Jace let out a slight grunt.

His pain must be terrible. "I'll go for help as soon as I can."

"Not yet. They know we're close with no place to go. They'll be patient looking for us."

Suddenly, the trapdoor opened.

Brynne pulled the trigger.

A thump echoed as the man stumbled backward. Did she dare stick her head out to see if she'd hit him, or would she be fired upon at close range?

Huck screamed and put his hands over his ears. "Too loud!"

Jace pushed the boy's head to his shoulder. "It's okay, son. I've got you."

Fergie barked.

So much was riding on her shoulders. *Please, God, be with us. Protect Huck and Jace. Help me make the right decisions this time.*

Jace cringed against the pain, as he fought to clear his mind. He got to his feet and set Huck on the concrete step. "Sit right there." He looked over his shoulder at Brynne. "Let me see if you caused any damage."

He didn't wait for a reply since he expected her to argue. Fergie shivered beside him, and he peeked over the edge of the baptistry. The lightning streaked, and he could see someone lying on the ground holding his shoulder. The man rolled over and struggled to get to his feet. Where was the other man? He turned and whispered, "You hit him."

Just as she stuck her head up, a shot blasted, splintering the wooden lid. They both dropped back down.

She said, "He's in the corner of the building. His gun is bigger than ours, and I'm pretty certain they have more ammunition between the two of them."

They were in a bad way. Brynne only had two more shots and with it being dark, the likelihood of hitting her target and taking him out was risky. The chances of them being hit by the men were more probable. The good thing was the men didn't know Brynne was short on ammo.

"I have to take him out."

"Wait." Jace eased upward. The injured man was no longer there. He and Brynne had to get out of here. Maybe they could take a chance.

Suddenly, footsteps crossed the floor. Brynne stood and fired off one shot.

The man hit the floor but came back up firing.

There was no way out. They were outgunned. "Brynne, I want you to protect Huck while I run for it. I'll find the deputies and give them our location." He grabbed an old piece of lumber and held it up. "I'll try to take one of them out."

"No," she snapped. "They'll shoot you. Huck and I can't stay here. We'd sitting ducks."

"We're trapped already. It can't get any worse."

Fergie again sat and barked.

Brynne jerked toward the canine. "She's trying to tell me something."

Jace looked at the dog. She was sitting in the water, even though it was freezing, and she stared at Brynne while she whimpered. "We'll check it out once we're safe."

He mouthed *okay* even though he doubted if all three of them would get out alive. A shuffle of feet sounded on the floor. The men were moving.

He had to go for it.

Jace shot to his feet. Shoving the pain to the back of his mind, he climbed the concrete stairs and raised the board. He prepared himself to be riddled by bullets, causing pain and being knocked to the ground. But it didn't happen as he hobbled across the floor.

Gunfire lit up the sky from outside the open door and one of the attackers fell to the floor. More shots, and then he caught a glimpse of someone in dark colors running away through the trees. "Let's go, Brynne. Run."

He took Huck from her, and they hurried out of the dilapidated church building, and he followed her. He struggled to keep up while carrying Huck but moved as fast as possible.

When they had gone several yards past the edge of the trees, she slowed and looked back. "Where are they?"

"I don't know." He turned around. A bad feeling came over him. "I don't see them."

"It almost seemed like there was someone else shooting. Like Dotson and the other deputies. Wait." She pointed. "Is that someone?"

He looked just as a figure melted between two trees and disappeared. "Looks like it. I saw someone, but being that he shot the kidnappers, it seemed like he was on our side."

"Like a deputy?"

"No. This guy looked to be dressed in all black, but I could be wrong." Jace held Huck close as he scanned the area. "We need to keep moving."

"Wait. There. I see him." She continued to stare. "There's something about the way he moves that seems familiar." She moved to the right, and then back to the left. "Where did he go?"

He shrugged. "I lost him."

She continued to stare. "I don't know who he is, but I'm glad he helped. Fergie was trying to tell me something. I need to see what she was barking about before we go."

"Can it wait? At least until the deputies get here?"

"It won't take but a sec. I want to know what she detected.

Watch for us." She led Fergie back into the building, and he stepped into the doorway.

Five or six seconds ticked by before she hollered, "Jace, come here."

Now that the gunmen were not shooting at them, the burn of his wound raged hot. He hoped whatever she'd found was important because they needed to find the others. But as he moved through the doorless entry, Brynne held a human skull.

"Fergie found a human skeleton. I have a hunch it's Carrie."

He drew a deep breath. If it was Carrie, then it was clear the danger tied back to her. All along he knew it could be true, but this changed everything. Someone had killed a seventeen-year-old girl and disposed of her body in a church building, of all places. "Let's find the deputies and get them on it."

"Already on it." She checked her phone and shook her head. "Still no signal. I hope we can find them on the other side of the woods. Come on."

He followed and struggled to keep up. Huck squirmed in his arms, and Jace tugged his coat around him again. "We'll get warm soon."

"I want to go home, Daddy. I'm cold."

"We're hurrying, son." As he headed through the trees, he wondered about the man. "I want to know who helped us. It definitely wasn't Sonny."

"That was my first thought, because the man was too agile." She sighed. "And it doesn't make sense. How did someone know where we were? And that there were two men attacking us. At the beginning it was just one."

"I don't know, but it makes me wonder if Sonny sent someone to follow you?"

She glanced at him. She shivered. "Don't even say that."

The snow was several inches deep now, and his thigh continued to throb. Moisture ran down his leg. Dread filled him at the thought of having to make it all the way back to the ranch.

A dog barked in the distance. He and Brynne looked at each other, then she yelled, "Over here."

They headed back toward the church building but met the deputies on the trail before they got there.

Dotson looked at Brynne and Fergie, before his gaze landed on Jace. "How's that wound?"

How did he think it was? Painful. But Jace kept the sarcasm from his reply. "I'm ready to get the bullet removed."

"I'm sure you are. After we saw where you disappeared from GPS, we took a dirt trail to the far side of the property. My SUV is not far."

Brynne said, "Lieutenant, we found human remains. Actually, Fergie was the one who found them."

Dotson's gaze narrowed. "Where was this?"

"In the baptistry of an abandoned church building. Did you pass a few buildings on the trail?"

"Yeah, we did."

Brynne gave an abbreviated version of holing up in the structure, being shot at and Fergie's find.

The lieutenant glanced over his shoulder at Deputy Randall. "We've got a long night in front of us. We need to contact Forensics, but we need to get y'all out of the cold first. The little fellow—" he nodded at Huck "—must be freezing. Then we'll take Jace to the hospital."

"If you can drop us off at my house, I can drive myself to town."

Brynne threw him a look without saying anything. Didn't have to. Jace knew she didn't approve of him driving him-

self, and she was probably right. But he didn't want to be
without his vehicle once he was released.

Ten minutes later, Jace sat in Dotson's Ford Expedition
with Huck fast asleep on his shoulder while Brynne talked
with the lieutenant. He laid his head against the headrest
and carefully stretched his leg. His eyes closed. In no time,
with the heater blowing full blast, Huck's warmth penetrated
through his shirt.

He'd almost lost his boy. How had assisting in searching
for a lost teen escalated into his boy being kidnapped and a
shootout with two men?

Something more was going on here.

Did it have to do with Carrie and Reagan, or Brynne?
After Sonny's warning, his gut told him Brynne was the
real target.

She'll stir up a hornet's nest.

TWELVE

Brynne shivered against the cold and glanced over her shoulder at the vehicle. She had been standing out here for the past ten minutes answering questions from the lieutenant. Couldn't they talk on the way to the ranch? She tried not to get frustrated, but she was concerned about Jace.

"Again, how did you get away from these men?"

She hadn't mentioned the man in black. She felt more comfortable telling the sheriff about the mysterious man than Lieutenant Dotson. She had seen the man for only seconds. She didn't know what to make of it and hated to answer the question, since it would bring on many more. But she couldn't lie, either. "We heard shots from outside. I don't know where they came from, but the heavier gunmen fell—he was shot. We ducked back down into the baptistry. When we came back up, there were more shots and the men fled."

"Did you see how they escaped? Were they on foot? Or perhaps a four-wheel-drive truck, or an ATV?"

"No. I didn't see anything. Earlier we had heard what sounded like an ATV. Did you see one at the edge of the woods when you came looking for us?" She found herself talking faster, hoping to get this conversation over with quickly.

"There was no ATV there."

"Then I assume that was the one we heard. Someone

must've gone back for it." She rubbed her arms and danced in the cold. "Can we go now? It's freezing."

"Sure. Just be ready to fill out a complete report tomorrow. We will have more questions for you."

She hurried around the vehicle and got in on the opposite side of Jace. Fergie was lying in the back, and according to the soft snores, she was asleep.

They waited another minute or two before the lieutenant strolled to the driver's side and climbed in.

Finally.

Brynne tried not to stare at Jace, but it was impossible. She was worried about him and little Huck. The boy was precious, and Jace was a caring dad. Not that that surprised her. She'd always known he'd make a good family man someday.

"Are you doing alright?" the lieutenant asked her.

"I'm fine." That wasn't really true. She was scared and confused. Scared for Jace, and everyone involved. Her gaze went to Huck. What had she gotten herself into? She had thought this was all about the missing teen and her mother. There was no doubt in Brynne's mind the skeleton belonged to Carrie. Did her killer believe Brynne could identify him? That had to be it.

"Are you certain you're okay?"

Again, she looked up at Lieutenant Dotson. "I guess I'm a little shaken up. It's been a long two days." Hopefully, he accepted the answer. She had to have time to think. It would help to have a good night's sleep. Rest. And time without being in danger to be able to put things in perspective. After she got Jace to the hospital, she hoped to move quickly. Surely, he would be safe in a hospital room with people all around. If Sam and his mother or Tessa could watch little Huck, she would have to investigate quickly.

A few minutes later the lieutenant pulled into Jace's

drive. As soon as the SUV stopped, Jace opened his eyes and looked around.

"We're at the ranch."

A slight smile covered his lips as he tried to sit up. "Yeah, I recognize it."

Inwardly, she smiled. Jace always had a sense of humor. She got the feeling he was going to need it. Sam strode out of the house. Jace had the door open before his brother got there.

Sam held out his arms. "I'll take the little guy."

Jace shook his head. "I can carry him." He climbed out of the vehicle with his son in his grasp and headed toward the house. Stubborn man. But Brynne should have known with the danger his son had been in he would not freely give him up so quickly.

"Thank you, Lieutenant."

"Brynne, don't forget to fill out that report tomorrow. Try to get some sleep and let your dog rest."

"Her name is Fergie." Annoyance went all over her. Her dog had found Huck, trekked across the countryside and found human remains. She detested how he constantly referred to her dog like she needed extra rest and care. But now would not be the time for a longer response because she was sure it would come out ruder than she intended. "Good night."

She hurried through the back door to see Huck in Sam's arms, and Jace leaning against the wall. Both of them looked at her and then exchanged glances.

"Did I miss something?" she asked.

Jace said, "Tessa can take me to the hospital."

She glared at him, trying to figure out what he was trying to do. She was perfectly capable of taking him herself. "No, thanks."

She looked at him and said, "Let's go." She turned and walked away without waiting for him to answer. She got into her truck, slammed the door and flicked the heat to high. In no time, Jace walked out of the house and climbed into the passenger side. Silence reigned as she put the vehicle into gear and took off. After she pulled out on the road, she said, "You don't have to protect me."

"Get off your high horse, Taylor. We were trying to figure out the best people to watch Huck. Sam is capable. But Tessa is still a tad shook up. We only thought it might help her to be away from the danger."

Well, now she felt like a heel. "Sorry. I didn't think about that."

Every bump the truck hit made Jace feel like his thigh was being stabbed with a knife. "Could you take it easy?"

"I'm trying," she snapped.

"Thank you for helping me back there."

"You're welcome." Her voice came out tender and concerned.

He must've dozed off because when he opened his eyes, they were pulling into the ER. A man and a woman opened his door and helped him into a wheelchair. The pain was even worse, making him push back against the seat. Brynne must've called ahead for them to be waiting on him. Minutes later, he was whisked into a room and put in a bed under a bright light above it. He didn't remember much after that, but seemed to recall them giving him pain meds. When he awoke, his leg was bandaged, and Brynne was sitting by his side.

"You stayed with me?"

"You're awake. Of course, I did. Even though you're a pain, I wouldn't leave you alone." Her amber eyes glistened.

His chest tightened as he glanced around the room. "Where's Huck?"

A warm hand touched his. "He's fine. He's with Sam,

Tessa and your mom. Loughlin assigned around-the-clock watch at your place."

He released a sigh. "That's a relief. I never would've survived without you."

"Without me? What about our mysterious helper?"

He'd forgotten about that. "My brain's a little fuzzy. I need to let it clear." Sleepiness tugged at him, probably from the anesthesia, and he hated it. He inclined the bed, hoping to wake up.

A slight headache tugged at Jace, but he needed to get out of here. As if on cue, a man in scrubs and a white coat entered the door. "Well, you look like you have company."

"Let me step out," Brynne said.

The doctor waited until she exited, then turned back to Jace. "How is your pain level?"

"Just a dull ache. But I'd like to leave the hospital as soon as possible."

If the man had any compassion, he didn't show it now. "You'll need to stay overnight for observation."

"I need—"

The man shook his head. "Maybe in the morning. I'm certain you have many things to do just like all of our patients. You have a bullet wound. The area will be tender, and to lessen muscle damage, you need to take care of yourself."

The man's tone made Jace feel like he was being lectured, and it would be of no benefit to argue.

"We'll get you moved to a regular room shortly. I will see you in the morning, and if you have no complications, I'll release you to go home."

"Thank you." Jace forced a smile as the doctor padded out of the room, but to say he was annoyed was an understatement. His instinct was to walk out of the hospital, but since his head was still swimming that might not be a good idea.

Brynne poked her head through the door. "Is it alright to come in?" At his nod, she stepped inside. "I take it was bad news."

He nodded. "The doc wants me to stay overnight."

She put her hand on his foot. "I'm sorry. I know you must be disappointed, but it's probably for the best."

He couldn't resist glaring. "I worry about you, Brynne. I took a bullet. Next time it might be you. I can't even protect Huck. And you think it's for the best?"

"I'm a law officer. It's my job to protect you, not the other way around." She smiled. "Guess I didn't do such a great job, huh?"

"You and Fergie are competent. You make a great team."

"Sure."

Jace's mind was on Brynne. Logically, he knew she was right, and it was her job to protect. No doubt, she was capable, but that didn't mean he had to like it. How would he ever forgive himself if something happened to Huck or her while he was lying in a hospital bed doing nothing? He and Brynne locked gazes. She knew he was feeling helpless, and yet, she made no argument for him to get out of here.

A few minutes later, an orderly came in and brought Jace to a regular room. While he was being brought to his room, Brynne went to her truck to get Fergie. She waited in the hallway until he was settled and then she came in and sat down in the lounge chair beside his bed. Fergie stopped beside his bed and looked at him with her tail wagging.

"Come on, girl. He's fine. Lie down," Brynee said and the dog sat at her feet.

A glance at the clock on the wall showed it was 1:45 a.m.

"You need to get some rest." She rested a hand on his shoulder.

He was completely exhausted, yet he didn't see how he

could sleep. Maybe the anesthesia was working on him. "Have you heard from Sam, or my mom?"

"Sam called about midnight. Everyone else had already gone to bed but he was keeping watch even though the deputy is stationed at the end of your driveway. He said everyone was fine. He wanted me to reassure you they have everything under control."

Jace eased his head back onto the pillows and closed his eyes for a second. "My family have been good at taking care of things." As soon as the words were out of his mouth, he realized his mistake. "I didn't mean anything by that."

"I know you weren't taking a shot at me. But you're right. You have a lot of support. Don't ever take that for granted."

She folded her arms across her chest, a telltale sign that her words contradicted her feelings. He reached out with his hand open, and she took it. He wasn't good at saying how he felt, but he tried. "I'm glad you're back."

"Are you?" She pulled her hand away. "Why didn't you contact me sooner?"

When he opened his eyes, she was staring at him with a mixture of hurt and anger.

"Because I was young and stupid. I listened to Sonny. My intention was to reach out immediately and keep my word."

"Sonny? What does he have to do with anything?"

Jace hated talking about this, but she needed to know. "He told me to let you get settled and that many kids struggle to move on with their life especially if people from their past won't let them get adjusted first. Saying the words out loud, I see how stupid it was." And he had been foolish to listen. Brynne had a trust issue and he just added to it. "I respected Sonny, and he'd been adamant."

"Why would you listen to him? You made a promise."

Jace looked up at the ceiling before turning back to her.

"He told me it was common for kids who were moved and didn't want to be, that they might go to extreme measures, like run away. He said then they would get in trouble with the law and be moved again. I had seen it before, so I believed him. There was a young kid, I don't remember his name, but he had run away from the Mooneys to go back home in Sulphur Springs. This was the third time he had run, and CPS put him in a special home that was for troubled kids where they went to school, almost like a compound."

She squinted. "And you think that's what I would have done? Run? I've had my troubles, but I don't thwart authority. Never have."

"I know." He tried to take her hand, but she pulled back, then settled it in her lap. Frustration bit at him. "I don't blame you for not wanting to have anything to do with me. Just believe me when I say I'm sorry. It's one of my biggest regrets."

For several moments, the room was silent with only the humming of his blood-pressure cuff as it came on. What did she expect from him? He regretted that he had hurt her. That had never been his intention. But he also knew Brynne. She had needs he'd never be able to meet. Maggie had proven that. What was he supposed to do, put everything on the line, including Huck, and hope she didn't take off just like Maggie? He couldn't do that again.

Several more minutes passed, and he thought she had fallen asleep in the chair.

"Don't feel bad. I can make it on my own." Her voice dropped even quieter. "I've been doing it my whole life."

THIRTEEN

Brynne left the hospital early Friday morning with the weight of the situation on her shoulders. Fergie's paws were a tad swollen. A quick visit to her veterinarian last night showed the damage was minimal and would heal after a couple of days of rest. She already felt like she was losing the race to prove her worth on the K-9 team, no matter how well her partner performed. If Loughlin retired and it was up to Dotson, she was afraid he'd desire Jeff Mayes and Boss on the team. Would the department give Fergie a chance to heal? Or would they be like Denver and not give her the opportunity because they'd be concerned she'd be hesitant to go back into danger? Or, worst of all, could it true that Fergie would be tentative to work? If so, that could be a risk if they were on a search-and-rescue mission.

And then there was Jace. She could feel the tension between them. The physical awareness when they accidentally touched. Or was it simply her imagination? No matter, now he had Huck to consider and the thought of him putting his life on the line for her didn't settle well in her stomach.

You're not worth it.

The little voice whispered in her head. Her stepdad had yelled it once at her while her mom stood by and listened. What had even made him angry, she couldn't remember. But his words had cut deep. If anyone else got hurt, Jace or a deputy or Fergie, others would blame her, even if they didn't vocalize it. Deep down, she didn't believe Jace would fault her, but she simply didn't know. Yearning for acceptance was her constant companion. Needing reassurance was not an attractive trait. She saw it in others and pitied them. She didn't want sympathy, but she didn't know how to rid herself of the feeling, either.

If only things had gone differently for her as a kid. Her parents had separated right before her daddy was killed in that car accident, when Brynne was six. It was possible if he hadn't died, he and her mom could've reconciled, and her mom wouldn't have married her stepdad. Just one thing that led to another. She tried not to feel sorry for herself or be dramatic, as so many people like to call it. The events of the past weren't anyone's fault, except for her stepdad. He'd been playing his video games and had the cords strung across the living room floor. A friend from school dropped by for a visit, and Brynne dashed through the house to answer the door, and she tripped over the cords, ripping them from the outlet. In a fit of anger, her stepdad shoved Brynne hard, knocking her into a bookshelf. When she complained to her mom about the pain, she told her to keep quiet and that it would heal on its own. Three days later, the school nurse called her into her office to ask her about her injuries. A trip to the emergency room showed she had three broken ribs.

Brynne did blame him for her being put into foster care. Her mom was also partly to blame.

If her dad had lived, Brynne liked to believe her life wouldn't have spun out of control. Her memories of him were few, but strong. Sometimes she wondered if he, too, would've let her down like so many others. Maybe it was her fantasy to believe how much he cared for her.

She glanced in the rearview mirror. Fergie was lying down in the crate. The Saint Bernard had been her best friend. Her partner could've easily been shot or injured while running around in the wilderness evading the gunmen. Enough dwelling on the past. Brynne needed to concentrate on this case before someone else got hurt.

The question was why.

It all had to be about Carrie and the father of Reagan. It was the only thing that made sense. Brynne only had until later today before Jace would be released from the hospital.

What to do? She didn't want to go home, and she hadn't been given any job duties except to go home and rest. That was out of the question. It was time to find out who Reagan's dad was. She pulled into the next parking lot, a floor supply place, and searched on her cell phone for Greg Crawford. He was the last guy Brynne remembered dating Carrie. He'd been a senior and loved baseball. A guy with a sense of humor who was friendly to everyone. There were several people with the same name in Texas, but she only found one with the right age. It looked like his last known address was in San Antonio. She wanted to check him out, but didn't know if she had time to visit him in person. It'd be about a five-hour drive one way.

She found a phone number for him and drew a deep breath. Should she call? If he answered, what would she say? *Hey, Greg, did you happen to be the father of Carrie's Kaufman's baby?*

The sheriff's words played back to her, reminding her she was part of a team. She called Sergeant Lancaster to inform him she was going to contact Greg. He agreed to add the man's name to the list of contacts, and she agreed to let him know how it went.

The sergeant said, "Before you go, I wanted to let you know

Forensics was at the crime scene this morning to recover the skeleton. There was a gold chain clasped in the hand."

It took a second for her to process the information. "So there's a possibility the chain belongs to the killer."

"I'd say so. I'll send you photos of it shortly. See if you recognize it."

"Thanks. I'll do that."

She disconnected feeling a little more hopeful. There wasn't a nonchalant way to broach the subject with Greg, so she just needed to be blunt. She hit the number and half hoped he wouldn't answer.

"Hello," a pleasant, feminine voice answered.

Brynne's stomach tightened. She hadn't expected a woman to pick up. "I'd like to speak to Greg Crawford, please."

The voice chilled a tad. "Can I ask who's calling?"

"This is Brynne Taylor from Hope Valley."

"Sure. Hold on." There was static before the woman said, "Go tell Daddy he has a phone call."

Brynne released the breath that she'd been holding. She hoped Greg was not Reagan's father, and if he was, that this didn't cause problems with his wife.

"This is Greg." He sounded out of breath, like he'd been exercising.

"Hi, Greg. This is Brynne Taylor. I don't know if you re-member me." Don't worry about his wife. Just keep this pro-fessional. If he was Reagan's dad, he would be a suspect in Carrie's murder.

"Of course, I remember you." His tone was jolly and didn't seem forced. "It's been forever. What can I do for you?"

"I need to ask you something…personal."

"Okay…" Birds sang in the background, as if he'd stepped outside. "Go ahead."

"I work with the Rockford County Sheriff's Department

now and am investigating a case. You dated Carrie Kaufman before she disappeared." She purposefully paused to get his reaction, but there was only silence. She continued. "She had a baby before she vanished. Is it possible you were the father? And would you agree to give us a DNA sample to confirm it?"

Suddenly the background noise disappeared. Had he gotten inside a vehicle or a garage to make certain he wasn't overheard?

"No way Carrie had a baby. I would've known. How can that be?"

He sounded sincerely surprised, and Brynne's heart went out to him, but she was still cautious that he could fake his response on the phone. "She had a baby girl three days before she disappeared. Carrie's teenage daughter was attacked at the old Mooney home. It's important we learn the identity of the father."

A few quiet seconds crawled by. "I'm one-hundred-percent sure I'm not the father, but I will take the DNA test if it helps with an investigation. It's always bothered me the way she disappeared."

"We'd appreciate that. There is a local place where you can leave a sample. I'll text you the address. The sooner, the better."

"I understand."

"Can I ask where you were last night?" She felt like she was a lawyer or investigator on one of those old law television shows.

He chuckled. "You are kidding, right?"

"I'm afraid not."

"I went to my son's basketball game with my wife and two younger daughters. We lost, fifty-two to thirty-eight. My son fouled out in the third quarter. It was a home game at Franklin Middle School. Then we went home, had Tater

Tot casserole for supper and put the kids to bed. I hope that answers your question."

"I appreciate it, Greg." She detected annoyance in his answer, not that she blamed him. She wanted to gather as much information as she could while she had him on the phone. "Since you're certain you're not the father, do you know who might be?"

"Not really. I only dated her a few times. I liked her a lot and was surprised when she agreed to go out with me. Carrie spent more time asking me to take her to the Treehouse at Big Sandy River than she did doing things with me. She just wanted to drive around and see other people."

The Treehouse was a well-known hangout in the woods where the teenagers would meet to drink, make out and sometimes do drugs. It supposedly got its name some fifty years prior, when a group of boys told their parents they were going to build a treehouse, when it was really just a tall pecan tree that they used to hide their booze. Brynne had only gone there once, since she was afraid of getting caught by the Mooneys or the police. She didn't realize Carrie went there. "Thanks, Greg."

"Taz Franklin hung out with Carrie. That's when I decided I was better off not dating Carrie. I hope you learn what happened to her. If someone hurt her or was responsible for her disappearance, I want them caught."

"Me, too." She disconnected and glanced out of the windshield at the trees, but not really seeing. Carrie dated Taz. Brynne hadn't realized that, either. Taz was a troublemaker Brynne had in her geometry class. His parents had money, but he struggled to be popular. He was only mediocre at sports, and it seemed the teachers were always warning him that he in was in danger of failing. Brynne got the feeling his parents stayed on his case and that he was a disappointment to them. That he could do better in everything he pursued. But then Taz got into trouble for breaking into the school and vandalizing the science lab. He was sent to an alternative school. She'd heard stories about him later being in more trouble with the law, but she couldn't recall the specifics.

As she pulled back onto the highway, she thought about her conversation with Greg. Or had he effectively thrown her off track? She was always leery of those who seemed to have all the right answers. She believed him when he told her where he was last night. He could've hired someone to do his dirty work, but that would be elaborate for a family man. Even though she had the morning off, she drove to the department and pulled into the parking lot. Jace was concerned about her safety, but she had no plans to put herself in danger—she needed to find out who was targeting her. Preferably before he got released from the hospital.

"Hey, what are you doing here?" Allison asked as she came through the door. Her gaze went to Fergie, and she rolled her chair across the floor to look at her. "Aw. Did she get hurt?"

Brynne nodded. "Her paws are sore. We're not doing much today, but I'd rather be at work than be at home."

"Oh, yeah. I don't blame you. I wouldn't want to be home when there's a guy who wants to kill you on the loose."

Brynne shot her friend a smile. Allison didn't always offer the most encouraging words, but Brynne didn't think it was out of malice. She went back to the office that she shared with Deputy Randall. Fergie lay down on her bed, which was in the corner. She leaned to her left side, but then instantly rolled to the other side. Brynne petted her gently across her back. "I'm sorry, girl. You must be awfully sore. You'll feel better in no time."

As she sat down at her desk, she fired up her laptop. She

was relieved Randall wasn't in the office, nor his Belgian Malinois used to track down fugitives and find drugs. The department also used his K-9 in search-and-rescue, but after Fergie joined the team, he was used less.

As the computer screen was loading, she filled her cup with coffee, craving caffeine. She wondered about the man who'd saved them in the abandoned church. Was he a good Samaritan? A local who'd noticed people on the property and decided to intervene. That made no sense. There would not be a reason for him to leave. When she returned to her desk, she noticed a text from Sergeant Lancaster. An image of a thick gold chain appeared on her phone. She enlarged it for a better view. Disappointment slammed into her as she didn't think she'd seen the chain before. Next, she searched for Taz Franklin in the database. A long rap sheet pulled up, consisting mainly of theft crimes and one domestic violence charge. But nothing in the last six years. A look at his Texas driver's license showed that he lived in the nearby town of Wagoneer. She looked up his street address and was surprised when she discovered that he lived in an upscale neighborhood.

A general online search produced his name on a career social-media page. It showed he had been an agent for a large insurance company for the last three years. His clean-cut hairstyle and business attire certainly made him look better than his last mug shot. But just because he might have got his life together, didn't mean he hadn't hurt Carrie years ago. She took a screenshot of his information. Since he was close, she wanted to visit him in person.

A glance at Fergie showed she was asleep on her bed. Brynne couldn't stand to wake her. No doubt she was exhausted after last night and her paws being sore would make it worse.

She walked over to Sergeant Lancaster's desk and gave him a quick update on Greg and about her plans to visit Taz. He told her they were still contacting the places where Carrie had worked and making a list of contacts.

"Have you learned anything more about Reagan's condition?" she asked.

The sergeant said, "Mrs. Hepburn said the doctors plan to ease her off her medications today, and we should be able to interview her in the morning if everything goes well. Did you have time to view the gold chain?"

"I did, but I don't think I've ever seen it before."

"Okay. I'll be in touch."

Brynne left his desk and headed back to the front desk.

"Hey, Allison." When the dispatcher looked up from her work, Brynne continued. "I have an errand to run. Can you keep an eye on Fergie for me? She's sound asleep."

"I'd love to. She's such a big softy."

Allison loved animals and was always her first choice to help with Fergie if needed. She reminded her that Fergie wouldn't need to be fed while she was gone, and then gathered her things. A few minutes later, she was in her truck headed across the county. Taz's profile hadn't listed whether he was married or not, but she figured he might be. Seemed like most people in their thirties were or had been, except for Brynne. As she pulled into the insurance company's parking lot, her cell phone dinged, indicating a text had come through.

She parked and then glanced at her phone.

Are you okay?

The left side of her mouth quirked as she confirmed she was good. Jace must be worried about her. She didn't mind him being concerned for her. She guessed he was getting restless in a hospital bed. She'd probably feel the same way.

Are you home?

She sighed. She was tempted to ignore his text until she had finished her interview with Taz, but guilt tugged at her.

No. I'm checking on a lead. I'll let you know how it goes in a bit.

She hurried out of the truck as soon as she hit Send. When she went through the glass door, she crossed over to the receptionist, whose desk sat in the middle of the room. A nameplate on the desk read Courtney.

"Hello, Courtney. I'd like to see Taz Franklin if he's in."

The young lady smiled, showing adorable dimples. "He's out of the office, but I expect him shortly. Can I leave him a message?"

Brynne glanced at the empty lobby. "I'd rather wait for him."

"Uh, sure. Have a seat. Can I get you a bottle of water?"

"No thanks." Brynne settled in the corner seat, where she could see people coming and going. She retrieved her iPad from her backpack and began reading over her notes again. A check to her phone showed no texts from Greg telling her he'd taken his DNA test yet. It was less than two hours since she talked to him. Patience wasn't her thing right now.

The entrance door opened, and an elderly lady walked in. She asked to talk to an agent about a claim. The receptionist called someone and then brought the woman down the hall.

There was one more guy Brynne knew Carrie had dated, but she couldn't recall his name. He was tall with red hair.

A cowboy type. A while back, their old yearbook had been loaded onto the internet and Brynne looked it up. But she didn't see the guy. Wasn't he in their school? She couldn't recall.

Maybe Jace knew. She texted him, but he didn't immediately answer back, so she decided to do more research on the guy later. Now, she'd decided to look at some of Reagan's social-media posts. It was amazing how much she favored Carrie. She had a lot of followers, and many seemed to be cheerleaders and football players. The school appeared small, but Reagan must've been in a lot of activities. Her family photos were pictures with her parents and a younger brother. In all of the photos, she was smiling. But was she really happy? Had Brynne made a good decision in leaving the infant at the fire station? The move had bothered her conscience her whole life, as she'd wondered what had become of the girl. By all appearances, it looked like Reagan had been adopted by a nice family.

If Reagan was content, why had she tried to find her biological mom? Curiosity, or something else? If Brynne had been adopted, she liked to think she would've loved to have a permanent family. Every time she thought about family, her mind went to the Mooneys. And then back to her mom and dad. And then to the other three foster families she'd lived with.

She tried not to think of her stepdad.

How would things have turned out differently if her dad hadn't died in the car wreck? Would her mom have taken better care of her? Recollections of her dad were very few.

A memory of him walking through the door and holding his hands out to her hit her. *Brynne-Brynne—Daddy's home.* And then she remembered helping him pull his boots off at night. He'd sit in his leather recliner and say, "help me,

Brynne", and then he'd hold his foot in the air. It was a tiny thing, but she felt important helping him.

She thought about him occasionally. What would he have thought of her being in law enforcement in the K-9 unit? She thought he'd be proud, but she really didn't know. Since he'd been in the military, she assumed there were similarities between the two occupations. Once her mom remarried her stepdad, Mom barely talked about her dad. Did Mom not care, or was she nervous to do so? Brynne didn't know.

"Ma'am, Taz is back in the office."

She looked up at the receptionist. She'd been so deep in thought, she hadn't heard the woman approach. Brynne stood.

"His office is down the hall, third door on your right."

"Thank you." Brynne headed down the well-lit hallway, trying to get her thoughts back to Taz and Carrie. The door was open, and she peeked in to make sure she had the correct office before stepping in. The man behind the desk was looking at his computer with his back to her. Just like in his social-media profile picture, he was dressed in nice business attire and his hair was neatly cut. "Taz?"

He glanced up, and after a second, a smile spread across his lips, and he stood. "Brynne Taylor. Come on in!"

She returned the smile and shook his outstretched hand. "Hello."

He gestured to the chair across from his desk. "Have a seat and tell me what this visit is about. Are you looking to insure your house or automobiles?"

"I'm afraid I'm here on police business."

His eyebrows went up in surprise. "Would you like something to drink? Water or a soda?"

"No, but thanks for the offer."

He sat behind the desk. Even though a slight smile lined his lips, a serious gaze hijacked his eyes. He took in the logo on her shirt and his eyes narrowed. "You work with Rockford County Sheriff's Department. What can I help you with?"

"Carrie Kaufman." She simply said the name, and searched his features, waiting to get a read on his reply.

His face showed nothing but concern. "I don't understand. She went missing, what? Almost twenty years ago. I haven't heard from her."

"Sixteen years, but I need to ask you questions about the time you two dated." Greg hadn't used the term *date*, but Taz would get the point.

"I saw her some the summer before she disappeared, but not much. We hung out at the Big Sandy River. She was going through some tough times. I don't know why I'm telling you this—no one was closer to Carrie than you."

Low shot. She decided to take the direct approach again. "What about her baby? Were you the father?"

"What baby?" His eyes searched her face, but there was something lying beneath the surface. Like fake surprise?

"Carrie delivered an infant girl three days before she went missing. But I think you knew that already." Brynne said the last statement with confidence, hoping to make him believe she knew Carrie told him about the baby.

He held up his hands. "I knew nothing. All I know is she didn't drink that summer, which was unusual for her. I assumed she didn't want to get caught drinking. I didn't ask questions. She was working for the law firm, and I figured being around them made her want to clean up her act."

Brynne had never seen Carrie drink, although she had smelled it on her breath a couple of times. She didn't want to learn things now about Carrie like that. She preferred to think of her as the nice sister who was good to her. Because she was. If Taz was trying to derail the conversation, it almost worked. She needed to get it back on track. "Could you have been the father of Carrie's baby?"

"No." His gaze went to the photo on his desk that showed Taz with a pretty blonde and an adorable toddler girl.

"Would you be willing to take a DNA test?"

He shrugged and the smile vanished. "If some kid is looking for child support, it ain't going to happen. I'll only oblige to a court order."

"Not child support. Carrie's daughter was attacked at the Mooney property. Do you know of any reason someone would want to attack Carrie's child?"

"Well, yeah." His tone had changed to sarcastic. "I guess because he's the daddy and doesn't want the child messing up his life."

A woman dressed in a pair of slacks and business blouse walked by, but paused momentarily at the door, then moved on.

Taz lowered his voice. "If you're thinking that's me, you're barking up the wrong tree, Taylor. My life is on the straight and narrow. I would never attack a child."

It was amazing how fast his demeanor had changed. Because he had too much to lose? Or because he was guilty? She climbed to her feet and handed him a business card. "Think about the DNA test. Right now, we're trying to eliminate suspects."

He followed her to the door and got close to her. "Listen, Brynne. I didn't father no kid. And if I did, I didn't find out about it until now. Don't mess with my life."

Brynne caught the threat. "Call me so we can mark you off the suspect list."

As she walked away, she could feel his eyes on her back all the way until she exited the door. Her heart was still beating fast when she got into her truck. Was he just scared, or was he already in over his head?

A check of her messages showed she'd received one from Greg saying he'd given the DNA sample. Good. At least that was good news, even if it took a while to receive the results. Also, she had two missed calls from Jace, but she'd check with him in a minute. As she pulled out of the parking lot, she called Sheriff Loughlin and let him know Greg had obliged to their request, but Taz had not. He agreed to see if they could get a judge to sign off on a warrant, but it was doubtful since they had no evidence tying him to the murder or the attacks.

Her adrenaline was high as she drove down the street. Would Taz be so ignorant to threaten her if he was the one who attacked Reagan and her? That seemed like it was asking for trouble. But criminals were not known for their calculated moves and smarts. At least most of them weren't.

She hit Jace's number, but it went to voice mail. "Hey, it's Brynne. I'm out of my meeting and noticed I had two missed from you. Just calling you back."

After she clicked off, she wondered why he didn't answer, unless he was sleeping. She hoped that was the case. Her stomach rumbled, reminding her she hadn't eaten today. She needed to get something, but she also wanted to get back to the station to check on Fergie. The dog was probably awake by now.

She pulled into a drive-thru of a chicken place and bought a chicken in a biscuit. Then she stopped by the J Hilton's Farm Store and bought some beef snacks for Fergie. As she traveled down the highway, she continued to think about Taz. She had hoped he would've changed for the good by now. Even though his parents appeared nice, it wasn't uncommon for kids to struggle during their teen years and as young adults. Brynne knew this better than anyone.

She kept a good watch in her rearview mirror and her

surroundings. Jace was concerned about her, and that she understood. The light turned red as she pulled to a stop behind a ready-mix concrete truck. The traffic was light, and she was ready to get back to the department to talk with investigators. Suddenly, her passenger window exploded as glass rained inside.

She hit the gas and swung around the stopped concrete truck. After looking both ways and seeing no oncoming vehicles, she floored it through the intersection. A glance to the right from where the shot came from showed no one with a gun. Where had the shots come from?

The thought that hung over her head was wondering what Jace would say. This was what he'd been afraid of. Great. In the middle of danger, her first thoughts were going to Jace. This was not the time to be thinking of him, but she needed to find the guy who was shooting at her.

It was too quick after leaving Taz's office for it to be him. Unless he'd called someone to shoot at her.

Jace paced back and forth in his room. Sam, Tessa, Huck and his mom had come by to check on him.

His brother folded his arms across his chest. "Sit down and relax, Jace. Brynne can take care of herself."

"I know that," he grumbled. "I hate sitting here. She's investigating on her own. It wouldn't bother me if this jerk hadn't targeted her."

Tessa walked over and slid her arm around his. "Brynne's always been a survivor and the sheriff's department takes care of their own." At his look, she asked, "Would you like me to go check on her?"

Yes. No. *He* wanted to make certain she was safe. "There's no need. It would only put you in danger again."

His mom held her head high and spoke with confidence. "You two are going to get through this."

Was she talking about them as a couple, or surviving being attacked? He didn't know, but it didn't matter. "I appreciate that."

Tessa said, "We're going to go unless you need something."

"I'm good." Jace shook his head. He turned to Huck. Chocolate ice cream covered his chin, making Jace laugh. "Hey, son. Did you enjoy that banana split?"

Huck gave him a big nod.

"I've got this." His mom hurried to wet down a paper towel and clean Huck's face and hands.

"Thanks for the banana split. It sure beats the hospital food." Jace smiled at his son. "Be good and listen to Grandma."

"I will."

Tessa kissed him on the cheek. "Take care of yourself."

Sam patted his shoulder. "Take care."

"Thanks." After all four of them stepped out of the room, he pulled back the covers to climb into his bed. His cell phone had gotten shoved under his pillow. When he retrieved it, he noticed he had a missed call from Brynne. His heart rate picked up a tad. He prayed she was only checking in. He called her back, but it went straight voice mail.

A bad feeling came over him.

He glanced at his clothes in the small closet. It wouldn't take him a minute to get dressed and get out of here. Once he checked on Brynne, he could go home if she wasn't in trouble.

As he quickly slid on his shirt, a knot formed in his stomach. He prayed she wasn't in trouble again.

FOURTEEN

She called Dispatch to report the shooting and was informed a deputy was on the way. She pulled into a drive and turned around. The cement truck had pulled through the intersection and kept going. A mother and child were headed for their car at the convenience store across the street. No other vehicles were in sight. She would've pulled up to the woman to make certain they were okay, but since someone was targeting Brynne, she didn't want to put others in danger.

Seconds later, Deputy Randall pulled in at the store, and she parked behind him.

He got out. "Have you seen the shooter?"

"No. But you can see my passenger window. The shot must've come from over there. I didn't see anyone."

"Okay. Let's look around." He headed in the direction she had pointed.

The woman and child were gone, but two more cars pulled up to the store. "We need to block people from going inside until we secure the area," Brynne said.

"I agree. Let me call for more assistance."

Brynne walked behind the store and peeked around the corner. There was a dumpster that was overflowing, and a bicycle leaned against the building. She walked back to Deputy Randall as two more deputies pulled up.

Randall said to her, "I want you to stick with me."

It didn't take long for them to cover the area. Deputy Ludlam found two spent shell casings on the ground between the convenience store and the house next to it. Deputy Randall talked to the store manager and learned the outside security cameras were not working. Brynne answered the deputies' questions. Since she hadn't got a look at the guy or his vehicle, there was not much to go on to search for him.

Again, the attack made no sense. Why attack her with people all around? Why was he after her? Did she know Carrie's killer? Would she recognize his face?

If the attacker was Reagan's dad, surely, he realized DNA analysis would be able to identify him. What good would it do to kill Brynne?

Brynne continued searching around the convenience store—the place she believed the man to have taken aim from. She was standing at the back of the store when she heard movement in the ditch nearby. With her gun ready, she moved cautiously behind the dumpster. She stayed low as she approached the ditch. Suddenly, from the adjoining parking lot, tires squealed.

A maroon van sped across the pavement and the back door slid open. A man with an assault rifle aimed his gun into the trees. She raised her gun. "Stop! Rockford County Sheriff's Department."

The man ignored her and rapidly fired toward a figure in the trees.

She fired two shots.

Then, as fast as the van came, it peeled out of the parking lot and was gone. She talked into her radio. "Shots fired. Man down. Again, shots fired."

Keeping her gun ready, she approached the area where she had seen the victim go down. She crossed the ditch and came up the other side. A person was lying on the ground holding his chest. She approached with caution, but as she neared the victim, she spotted his weapon several feet away. She holstered her gun.

He was wearing a mask, and she kneeled beside him. His hands clung to his blood-soaked chest.

She swallowed down the tightness in her throat. "I am Deputy Brynne Taylor."

"I know who you are." His voice was weak and gurgled.

She removed his mask. He looked vaguely familiar, but she didn't know who he was. Blood drooled from his mouth. "Who are you?"

"You're… You're in danger. I got the wrong girl."

Confusion at his words didn't stop her from questioning him as his face turned ashen gray. "What do you mean the wrong girl? You mean instead of Reagan?"

Deputy Randall came up behind her, but she ignored him for the moment as she leaned closer to the man.

"I… I'm sorry." His eyes closed. The smell of peaches still lingered on his breath.

"Wait. Who are you talking about?" She grabbed his wrist and felt for a pulse. "No. No. No." She put her hands to his bloody chest and started compressions.

"Taylor. He's dead. He has an open wound in his chest." Deputy Randall tried to pull her away, but she couldn't stop.

"He's got to live." She had to keep trying. "What girl? Reagan or Carrie?"

"He's gone."

"Who killed him?" Tears lined her eyes. She stood and glanced down at her bloody hands and then back to him. "There's no doubt this was the man who attacked me years ago. But I don't know who he is. He says I am still in danger. Why would he warn me? What does that even mean? By who?"

Randall said, "I don't know. We'll find the answers."

She took a few steps away and gave the other deputies room to approach the victim.

When Lieutenant Dotson approached, he said, "He's a police officer with Wagoneer. That is Henry Fritz."

Brynne's head swirled. Henry Fritz. The name sounded familiar, but she did not know him. Disappointment tugged at her. She had always thought she would recognize the man who had attacked her the night Carrie disappeared. But she remembered working on a case or two with the Wagoneer Police Department and thought he did look familiar. Or maybe she had just seen his picture in the paper or something. "Lieutenant, why would a police officer attack me?"

"Excuse me?" Dotson pressed his lips together in a flat line. "Are you saying Fritz attacked you? When?"

"This is the man who attacked me the other day at the Mooney place, and I believe also the one who was there the night Carrie disappeared."

"You must be mistaken, Deputy Taylor."

"No, I'm not." Normally, she wouldn't argue with her superior, but this was too important. She shook her head as she tried to wrap her mind around the knowledge.

"Why do you think that a man who attacked you years ago is the same man who attacked you over the last couple of days?"

"The night Carrie disappeared, I was hit on the head and thrown into the tack room. That night I smelled something on my attacker's breath. Later, I realized it was peaches. But now after snacking on them a couple of times, I think it was peach rings—the gummy candy." As she watched the expression change on the lieutenant's face, she realized she would have to convince him. But she didn't have time right now for that.

"We will look into it." He raised his voice to speak to the group in general. "I want a background check done on Fritz. His DNA needs to be checked against Reagan Hepburn. Let's test the gun and the ammunition and compare it to other crimes used in the area. Everything we can find on this guy—should be easy since he's an officer with the Wagoneer Police Department."

"Does this mean Brynne is out of danger?" Deputy Randall asked.

"Maybe, probably not. We need to find out who was working with Fritz since there were two gunmen in the woods and who killed him."

"Lieutenant, before he died, he said he got the wrong girl. I believe I am still in danger."

He looked at her seriously. "I hope you're wrong."

Deputy Randall joined in. "The men who took out Fritz used an assault rifle. Almost looked like a hit." When the lieutenant scrutinized him, Randall shrugged.

"Fritz told me I was still in danger." Her throat closed around the words, making it hard to spit them out. "I was the target."

"Now, or back when Carrie disappeared?"

"I don't know." Actually, she felt as though she didn't understand anything right now, except this was more than Reagan's biological father coming after the teen because he didn't want to pay child support or whatever.

Overcome with weakness and uncertainty, she walked toward her truck. But if she was the target, then why had Reagan been attacked? It made no sense. She felt more afraid now than she had earlier while under gunfire. She wished Jace was here. She couldn't believe she was thinking this, but it was true he was the only person holding her to the past. And she needed someone who understood her. She had not misunderstood Fritz's comment. The question was, what did it mean for her now?

Jace sped down the highway. His thigh still throbbed, but not as bad as when the bullet had still been embedded in his leg. But he had gotten a message from Brynne just a few minutes ago. Even though she did not say it, she was scared.

She was going back to the department to gather Fergie and then head to her house. It took some arguing, but he finally convinced her to go to the ranch. Even though he'd visited with his family hours ago, he had called his brother to see if they were safe and he said they were fine. He was almost tempted to send them out of town to keep them safe, but he didn't want Huck that far away from him.

His mind spun as he could not get to Brynne fast enough. Time slowed to a crawl. When he finally arrived at the ranch, he shoved his truck into Park and hurried inside. He found Brynne pacing the floor with Fergie resting on her dog bed in the guest bedroom. He hurried over and pulled her hands into his. "Are you okay?"

"I just don't understand."

His chest felt heavy, but one thing he knew was that he had to get her away from here. "Let me take you somewhere safe."

Amber eyes looked up into his. "What good would that do? I'm the target. Whoever wants me dead will just wait until I return. Besides, I am a deputy and it's my job to help find this guy and bring him to justice."

"I knew you would say that." And he understood what she was saying. "You might not be wrong, but you could give the department time to find this guy without you constantly having to look over your shoulder."

She rubbed her head like she had a headache. "I'm just so tired. I would love to lie down and sleep for a week and not have to look over my shoulder, like you said. But how can I really do that and ever relax as long as this guy is out there? I don't know where to start anymore."

With Fergie watching them, he took her hand and led her to the barrel chair for her to sit. "Brynne, I won't leave your side until this guy is caught. I promise you that."

"I can't let you do that. You have your son to think about." She pulled her hands back to herself and got up. "I can't relax. I just need a little time to think this through."

He still cared deeply about her. She had had a rough time of it as a child and a teenager. She had seen so many things that most people didn't in a lifetime. He needed to make certain he kept Huck safe also. He could not afford to let someone take his son again.

Despite her words, she sat on the edge of the chair. "I have no idea which way to turn."

"Pray about it. I know I have."

"You're right. Good advice." She closed her eyes. Whether she was praying or just resting, he didn't know.

A few minutes later, she was still lying there. He knew she wasn't asleep yet, but she would be soon if she continued to lie there. He needed to help her figure this out.

He sat in the chair and simply watched her for several minutes, remembering back to when they would spend their days together. A desire to protect consumed him.

"Would you please quit staring at me?" Her eyes remained closed.

He smiled. "Just get some rest."

"I will try. Hard to do with an audience."

Only a couple minutes later, her breathing smoothed out, and he knew she was asleep. Silently, he got up and gave her a kiss on top of her head. Then he moved to the kitchen. Sam, Tessa and his mom were sitting at the table quietly visiting.

His mom said, "Huck and Liam are taking their naps."

"Brynne fell asleep, too." He told them everything Brynne had told him, from her visit with Taz to talking to Greg Crawford. "The sergeant said he was looking into potential men who could be Reagan's father. They are also looking at everyone Carrie worked with. Not just students that she dated in high school. But I wonder if they were barking up the wrong tree."

Sam frowned. "I agree with you. Sounds like there is someone else involved."

"Would a man really go to all this trouble just to keep his identity as a father secret?" His mom looked doubtful. "Killing a girl, and attacking several others?"

"Depends on his position or his career," Sam added. "Since Carrie worked at the law office, the father could be someone with power instead of just a high-school kid."

"Or the man could have a family that he's afraid of losing," Tessa said matter-of-factly. "I'm assuming the department is doing a DNA test on Henry Fritz to see if he's the father."

"Brynne said so." Jace's phone rang, and he picked it up on the first ring. He stepped into the living room for privacy. "Hello."

"This is Sonny. I heard about the attack on Brynne. Was she hurt?"

Suspicion hit him. "How did you hear that?"

"I have a scanner and sometimes I'll listen to law enforcement. Anyway, is she okay?"

"She sustained no injuries. Is there something you're not telling me?"

"I'm just concerned about the girl. She has always been very special to me and the missus."

"There's nothing to worry about. The gunman was killed." Jace purposely didn't mention Fritz's name. He wanted to see what Sonny knew already. It was curious to him that the man had warned them away from the case and now Brynne had been attacked again. He didn't like where his thoughts were going but he couldn't help it.

"That is good news. Let me know if you learn anything more. I will be praying for Brynne."

"Sonny." Jace tried to stop him from disconnecting.

"Yes?"

"You warned Brynne not to get involved. Did you know this was going to happen?"

Silence stretched out for several seconds. "I was afraid this was going to happen. Take her away from Hope Valley. I wish she would've never returned."

Jace stared at the phone after he disconnected. Sonny did not ask the identity of the gunman. Coincidence? Or did he already know?

Had Sonny paid the gunman to take out Fritz? The question came to Jace unbidden. There were two men in the woods last night, plus the man who helped him and Brynne.

If Sonny wouldn't tell Jace what was going on, maybe Celine would.

He walked back to the room to where Brynne was asleep. He hoped she slept well, for he did not believe the danger was over. There were too many unanswered questions and too many people that were involved. There was still the mysterious man who helped them, and Sonny knew too much. And most of all, Henry Fritz told Brynne he had got the wrong girl.

How much had Brynne told Sheriff Loughlin? Jace knew she didn't trust Lieutenant Dotson because of his dislike toward Fergie, but what about the sheriff? Could she trust local enforcement?

He was tempted to give the sheriff a call to discuss the case. Jace and his parents had lived in the area all of his life, and Loughlin had been sheriff for fifteen years. He'd heard nothing but good about the man.

No wonder Brynne was struggling with the case. There was simply nowhere to turn and not enough clues to figure out how to handle it. But like he told her, he would not leave her side until this thing was over.

As he listened to Brynne's even breathing, he couldn't decide whether to talk to Sheriff Loughlin about Sonny Mooney behind her back. What if Jace was wrong? Could he take the chance?

He had no choice.

FIFTEEN

Brynne opened her eyes to an unfamiliar room, something feeling off. Sunlight poured through a window onto the carpeted floor. Her heart raced as she tried to get her bearings. Then she recognized she was in Jace's house. The panic subsided, but it was short-lived.

Henry Fritz.

The memories of the van pulling up and firing, and Henry Fritz falling to the ground shot in the chest. *I got the wrong girl.*

The memories assaulted her, reminding her that danger was still close. So close she felt like she could reach out and touch it. Why had a police officer attacked her? Why attack Reagan? Why had he killed Carrie sixteen years ago?

Because he was supposed to have killed Brynne?

It made no sense. Why would anyone want her dead? She had simply been a teenager who had been moved from foster home to foster home until she landed at the Mooneys'.

Sonny Mooney had to be the connection. Had she been betrayed by her foster family?

But why? Simply because they hated her? That made no sense. Certainly, there was no money involved where she was concerned. She had none. Revenge. Revenge for what? She hadn't wronged them in any way. There simply was no reasonable explanation. But if she could figure out the reason, maybe it would lead her to the men who killed Fritz.

And to the person or people who wanted her dead.

She thought back to the day that Carrie disappeared, and once again her memories would not allow her to forget dropping baby Reagan off at the fire station. Was someone after her because she gave the baby away? Could it be Reagan's daddy, and he was simply mad because she had given the baby away? Maybe the dad did not know he was a father until it was too late, and Carrie had agreed to give the child away instead of keeping her. It seemed far-fetched to Brynne, but she simply had no other explanation.

Or maybe it was the father's family. The father's mom or dad. A grandparent angry enough to kill.

No one hated her that she knew of. Well, except for maybe her stepdad. Did he blame her for being put into foster care because of the medical neglect caused by her mother not turning him in after he had broken Brynne's rib? He'd only spent one night in jail before he was let out on bail and was given probation. In her opinion, her stepdad had gotten off easy, but it was possible.

How long would it take Sergeant Lancaster to check him out? As much as she didn't want to admit the anger he'd exhibited to her when she was a child, she needed to know if he had connections to Fritz.

Memories played over and over through her mind like a video on autoplay. Carrie's blood on the barn floor. The smell of peaches on hot angry breath. The man warning Brynne not to tell anyone about his presence, or he would hurt Tessa. Being dragged into the dark tack room and being hit over the head.

"Did you get some sleep?"

The loud voice made her jump. "Jace Jackson, you scared me half to death."

"I didn't mean to startle you." He stood in their doorway, probably giving her some room, since she had overreacted. "I talked to Sheriff Loughlin. Hope you don't mind."

"I wish you'd let me be a part of that conversation. What did he say?" She climbed to her feet and stretched. Every muscle in her body was tight, and her shoulders and neck ached with tension.

"The investigator talked with Reagan."

"Please, tell me you learned something." She brought her hands together to her chin.

"She admitted she and a friend did DNA ancestry search when they read an article about a guy who'd learned he was related to a famous rock-star singer. She was shocked to learn her parents weren't her biological parents and set out to find out who were her real parents. She found the connection to Carrie but was also searching for possible matches for her dad."

"Was it Fritz?"

He shook his head. "No. The investigator is still checking things out, and the sheriff didn't have any specifics yet, but they're working on it."

"I wish they could move faster." Something delicious wafted to her. "What's that smell? I haven't eaten since breakfast."

"Mom made chocolate-chip cookies. Would you like some?"

"Yeah, give me a minute." She made a quick trip to the restroom and splashed water on her face, trying to shake the cobwebs. Then the smell of the cookies led her into the kitchen, where Jace was pouring a cup of coffee. He shoved it across the counter to her and removed a plate from the microwave. "Do you need juice or milk also?"

"A small glass of milk sounds perfect. This will do. I'm

starved." She noticed his limp as he put a pan in the sink. "I almost forgot, how is your leg?"

"Sore and stiff. I'm sure it will be for a couple of days, and hopefully my doctor will still see me after me skipping out on him today."

"You didn't have to do that for me, you know."

A lopsided grin crept up his face. "I care about you, Brynne. I don't mind."

She didn't respond to the statement. But with everything coming at her from seemingly all directions, it was nice to hear the words. "Did you notify the doctor or nurses before you left? Is there a hospital staff searching for you?"

"I told Kelsey, my nurse. She wasn't happy and scolded me."

Jace cleaned the kitchen while she ate the delicious cookies, feeling much better. He didn't say a word and probably realized the quietness had many helpful benefits. She got up and rinsed her dishes in the sink, then put them in the dishwasher.

A door slammed in the back part of the house, and a kid yelled. Jace said, "Huck and Liam must be up."

"Sounds like it."

She stared at him for a moment, wondering if she should even broach the subject. But at a time like this, she felt it was important. "Remember how I told you the man in the barn had threatened me if I told anyone he would not only hurt me, but my little sister? Meaning Tessa."

"Sure." He shrugged like he was waiting for her to continue.

"Do you think Fritz meant that Tessa was the target?"

"I don't think so." His eyes narrowed. "But he did hit her when he took Huck. Or one of the men working for him hit her."

"Yeah. But I'm not certain it fits, either. I just don't want to be so focused on one thing that I miss what's right in front of me. Right now, I don't feel like we can rule out any suspect."

"I agree." Jace looked at her as his eyes searched her face. "What bothers me is who would want to shoot a police officer and why. What was Fritz involved in? And more to the point, what was he involved in sixteen years ago?"

"Fritz couldn't be much more than a rookie at the time. I would like to look into it." It felt good talking with Jace about the case. Made her not feel quite so alone. "I'm worried about Huck. And about Tessa. Do you think we would be better off sticking all together? I don't know if that would offer protection or if it would make us a bigger target."

"I'd rather stick together."

She went over Fritz in her mind and tried again to remember the night Carrie disappeared. The threat. The smell of peaches on his breath. She had caught him in the act of killing Carrie, no doubt. And now, she knew he was getting rid of her body. She voiced her thoughts. "It makes sense now, kind of, I must have interrupted him getting rid of Carrie's body. The rest of the family was gone. There was blood on the floor, which meant Carrie was probably already dead. Now that we know her body was in the old church building, it makes me wonder how he got her there. I would think it would be difficult for him to transport her there in his truck because the building is hard to access."

"I've been thinking about that, too. He was a police officer so he would not want to be tied back to her death."

"Right. And even back then, DNA was becoming a big thing and could easily tie back to him. Maybe that's why he didn't want to use his vehicle, besides it being difficult to drive that way. Then how did he get her there? It wouldn't have been on a horse."

"Didn't the ranch have an ATV at the time?" Jace asked.

"Yeah, you're right. If Fritz was the one to kill her, it made sense. Not all of it, but at least the way he carried it out. He was in the middle of killing Carrie, and I interrupted him. But how did he get the wrong girl? If he meant me, I wonder what made him want to harm me in the first place."

"He had to have been hired." She and Jace stared at one another for several long moments.

"I wonder if it was my stepdad. I don't know why he hated me so bad. I didn't live with him any longer, so why go after me then?"

Sympathy crossed his face, and he moved toward her and wrapped his arms around her. "I'm sorry, Brynne. We still don't know it was him because I have a hard time picturing a police officer being bought off by a man like that. We need to look into Fritz's background to know what someone had on him."

"Is it okay to come in? I wanted to get the boys a snack." Tessa stepped into the room, and Huck ran to Jace with his hands up.

"Daddy."

"Just discussing the case. Hey, son." Jace picked him up and gingerly tossed him into the air, catching him again.

Huck giggled.

For the next hour or so, Brynne made some phone calls and researched Henry Fritz online. At the time Carrie had gone missing, Fritz had only been a police officer for two and a half years. He had been raised thirty miles away in another county, and his family had been in the area for generations. She had tried to talk with his supervisor but had gotten nowhere. She called Sheriff Loughlin, and he informed her that he was already looking into it. Not only Henry Fritz, but they were also talking to people Carrie had worked with at the diner at the time of her disappearance.

"How's it going?" Jace walked into the room. His limp was not quite as pronounced.

"You're walking better."

He smiled. "That's the pain meds working."

She went on to explain about what she had found and what the sheriff had told her. "I guess I should feel better that they are investigating for me."

"I know it hasn't been long, but you have not been attacked since Fritz's death."

"I noticed that, too," she said. "I don't want to read too much into that. I wish he could've finished telling me what he meant. Besides, someone shot him and did not want him talking to me. I realize it could be anyone from his past and it could have nothing to do with me, but I don't think so." She caught the concern in his look. "What is it? What are you thinking?"

"Sonny Mooney bothers me. He's hiding something from us."

"I agree. It may be more than coincidence that both attacks happened on his place. I hope I'm wrong because the Mooneys meant the world to me."

Jace frowned. "You don't think he could be the father of Carrie's baby? He was never flirtatious with any of the girls that lived in his house. Right?"

"No way." She shivered. "He was never inappropriate with anyone that I know of. Like I said, he was a good father figure. And he didn't seem any closer to Carrie than he did the rest of us."

"That's what I thought, too. But I had to ask." He looked up at the ceiling, as if thinking. "If that's not it, then what does he know?"

Jace's mom came into the room, and he said, "Mom, you lived beside the Mooneys for years. Did anything ever seem strange about him and his wife?"

"Not at all. He was a very good neighbor. Sometimes the kids were rambunctious, but your father and I didn't mind. It was nice hearing the children play. Through the years, some of the kids had more trouble than others and not all turned out with happy endings. Sonny and Celine did what they could."

Jace's mom backed up what she believed. If the couple had been truly caring, why did Brynne have the feeling Sonny knew exactly why she was being targeted?

Was he involved? If so, why?

Jace paced the floor, tired of being around the house. He felt like they were waiting for something bad to happen. It grated on his nerves. Tessa and his mother baked cookies, and if the smell wafting through the house was an indication, they had put on a roast for supper.

Sam came into the living room. "Would you like some help feeding the animals?"

Brynne glanced up from her iPad. "I can do that. That way you and Jace will not be at the same place in case we're attacked again."

"Let me go." Jace held his hand out to Brynne, then turned back to Sam. "You're right. I'm getting a little restless in the house."

His brother looked at him. "I still think it would be safer if I helped you. No offense, Brynne, but you seem to be the target. If someone is waiting for you, they can pick you off as soon as you're out the door."

Jace walked over and put his hand on her shoulder. "I think Sam is right. We just need to stay put."

Brynne sighed heavily. "This is getting on my nerves. I'm ready to hear from someone. Good news. Bad news. Anything is better than waiting."

He cocked his head at her. "I just want you to be safe."

The glare she shot at him made him chuckle. "We'll be right back."

Huck ran out of his bedroom and over to Brynne. "Would you like to play with me?"

"I would love to." She smiled at his son before she shot Jace one last scowl.

He and his brother walked outside while keeping an eye out for anything suspicious. Jace had not failed to notice the bulge under Sam's shirt in his waistband. He had never seen his brother carry, but if there was a time to be cautious, it was now.

They each grabbed a bale of hay and removed the twine from it. It was good to get a little exercise and burn off his pent-up energy. After they had divided up the hay between the horses, Sam put one boot up on the last rung of the fence. "I want you to be careful, brother."

"You know I am." Did Sam really think he had to warn him? Jace was getting tired of looking over his shoulder.

"I'm not just referring to the danger. I realize Brynne did not ask for this, nor did you. But I'm more concerned about you—about you falling for her again."

Jace busted out laughing. "I know what I'm doing."

"Tessa and I never did take to Maggie, but you probably knew that already. You and Brynne made a good couple, and I assumed you two would get married someday. But that didn't happen when she left."

Jace stared at him. His brother never offered advice and tended to mind his own business, so this was a surprise. "Just spit it out, Sam."

"You two have been through a lot, and I could easily see you two back together. My only advice is if you don't think it'll work out in the long term, back away. Brynne has been through enough."

"Are you being serious? You think you have to protect her from me?"

"Tessa mentioned it. She's always been concerned about Brynne. She looked up to her, but you know that. If you think you two have a chance, I support you. Go for it. But if not, back away."

Jace stared at Flash and Doo as they munched on their hay. He couldn't believe his brother would warn him away to protect Brynne. Did he really believe that he would hurt her? That was ridiculous. He had said Tessa was concerned. About what? That Jace would lead her on? There was no way. He had never confided in his brother about Sonny's request. They just didn't understand.

"Jace!" Brynne hollered from the house.

His heart tightened in his chest as he rounded the barn with Sam right behind him. When his eyes landed on her, she didn't seem to be in distress. He glanced around to make sure no one was targeting her. As if she realized the careless move, she stepped back into the doorway. Seconds later, he hurried through the door. "What is it?"

"I just heard from Sergeant Lancaster. Big news. Henry Fritz's wife admitted his gold chain had been missing for years, and after a look at her social media page, investigators found a photo of the couple with him wearing it. That places Fritz at the old church where Carrie was buried. It's believed he came after Reagan because she was asking questions, and he was afraid the body would be found. Thankfully the sale of the Mooney property hadn't gone through to Fritz or his secret may've remained hidden forever." She drew a deep breath. "Even bigger news. Using familial DNA search, they learned Reagan's father's identity. Mark Stowe."

"The state representative?"

"The one and only. It was the representative's first year in office."

Jace couldn't believe it. "No wonder Carrie didn't tell anyone. And that would explain why the representative wouldn't want anyone to find out."

SIXTEEN

Brynne looked at Jace. "We need to find something that ties back to Representative Mark Stowe. Since Sonny appears to know something, can we look in his house for clues? Do you think the Mooneys would mind?"

"Sonny already gave me permission to search the house and the authorities, which would include you. Maybe the deputies missed something. It's fine."

She loaded Fergie into his truck and then got in. When Jace shut his door, she said, "I feel like we're getting close to the truth. If we can find a clue to either Carrie, Fritz, or the representative in the house, it would go a long way. I'm ready for all of this to be over."

He smiled at her, exhaustion showing in his eyes, and it was obvious he hadn't shaved in several days. "I am, too. Brynne, I know it's been under extreme circumstances, but I've enjoyed spending time with you. I would like to talk when all this is over."

Her heart hurt. So many memories in the last few days. Finding Carrie's body. Jace being shot. The stress of trying to prove Fergie's skills to the lieutenant. Everything seemed to pull on her emotionally and it drained her. But at the same time, it was nice to spend time with Jace. It did not mean their relationship had to change. "It's been nice having you on my side."

"Way to keep it professional." His brown eyes connected with hers and she looked away. He could always read her mind. Not this time. Even though she was tempted, she knew it was not a good thing to open her heart up again. She might regret that someday, but how could someone open their heart again to such pain? Even with someone as handsome as Jace, and as sweet as his little boy was. If it didn't work out…

He pulled into the drive and cut the engine. His hand reached out and gave hers a squeeze. "Like I said, we can talk later."

But she wouldn't be able to give him what he wanted. She knew that now. He needed someone he could depend on, someone who could become a mother to Huck and not have doubts like she did. It was time to move on and close this case. "Let's do this."

He gave her one more glance before he climbed out of the truck.

As she let Fergie out, her hand still tingled from his touch. She tried to ignore the feeling that she was making a mistake with Jace. That she would regret it if she walked away. But this case took precedence right now. She walked up the porch steps and memories flooded her. She didn't know if it was nostalgia or simply the only place that had given her hope. She walked through the door and looked around at the surroundings. Most of the decorations were gone even though there were a few pieces of furniture still scattered about. No doubt, the rest of the furnishings had gone to their new home. With their new house being smaller, there wouldn't be enough room for everything. It made her sad to see the home deteriorate. People come and go. They buy a home and fix it up to raise a family. Then the children leave, and the people grow old. The circle of life played out in front of her.

"I'll check out the master bedroom," Jace said as they walked down hallway. "I would imagine they took most of their things, but I will check out their closet to see if any boxes or things are left on the shelves."

"I'll look in my bedroom." As soon as the words were out of her mouth, she realized her mistake. It was no longer her bedroom and hadn't been for years, but it was hard to get used to that idea. She climbed the stairs and noticed the nick on the stair railing that had been caused by her and Carrie horsing around. Brynne had taken a note some guy had given Carrie out of their room like she was going to read it. Carrie yelled at her to stop and threw a hairbrush at her. The brush hit the rail, leaving a mark, then both of them calmed down. When she walked into their old room sadness descended on her. It had been painted a girly pink when they lived there. She and Tessa shared a bunk bed. Tessa had slept on top. Carrie, being the oldest, had a bed to herself. They had each been able to pick their favorite bed cover. Brynne and Tessa had agreed to match and chose a solid color yellow with pink and purple pillows. Carrie picked black zebra stripes and concentrated her decoration efforts on the posters that hung above her bed of the latest teen craze.

Now, looking at the gray walls, it was difficult to tell this had even been a girl's room. The flower-shaped ceiling fan had been replaced with a generic white one, now covered in dust. The pastel multicolored curtains had been replaced with black plaid ones. It was no surprise the closet was empty, with nothing left of the lives they had spent there. The only piece of furniture left was a nightstand—new and cheap, like something from a bargain shop.

Brynne had not kept up with the kids who'd lived in the

house after she had been moved away. She would have to ask Tessa about that. Had Tessa remained in the room once Carrie and her were gone? She walked into the hallway and hollered downstairs. "I'm going to look in the attic."

Jace walked out of the master bedroom and looked up at her. "Okay. There were some tubs in the tack room. I am going to check them out. Let me know if you find anything or need help moving stuff around or going through things."

"Come on, Fergie." They climbed another set of stairs up a narrow hallway to the attic. Emptiness filled her senses, and the wind whipped through the house, making it creak. Boxes were stacked in the corners and all over, leaving just a small pathway through the middle. A lamp set to the side and a few boxes marked *bills*. She moved those out of the way, to see what was in the back of the attic. A couple of old lanterns, a box of quilts and a couple of out-of-date flower arrangements that were covered in dust. She opened the box of quilts and dug through, hoping she would find her old bedspread. But there was nothing that looked familiar. She scooted it out of the way and continued to dig through more boxes. One was marked Dolores, and another Caitlin. Brynne didn't know either girl. She moved and reshuffled bins and boxes, ready to find something that would connect Mark Stowe to Carrie. Would there be anything left at the law firm from when Carrie interned there for that summer? Hopefully the sheriff's department could obtain a search warrant to check it out.

Finally, at the bottom of a stack of bins, one had Brynne's name written on it. Curious, she hurried to remove the other boxes and opened the lid. There wasn't much inside except for a few T-shirts and an old jewelry box she barely remembered that had nothing valuable inside of it. At the bottom was a manilla envelope. When she opened the envelope, several photographs fell out. Three of them were of Brynne with her other foster siblings. One with her and Carrie. Another with her and Carrie and Tessa and their foster brother, Ricky.

Another stack of photographs showed some with her and the horses, and even one with her and Jace. She didn't remember seeing the photo before. A small smile crept across her face. He had been such a big part of her life back then.

The next image made her heart stutter. It was a military picture of her dad with his arm around Sonny Mooney. Her mind scrambled to figure out how this could be. Her dad had been in the army with Mr. Mooney. And Mr. Mooney never mentioned it? The last picture was of her dad in his squad of nine soldiers, the same one her mom had. Brynne had seen it when she was a little girl before her mom put it away.

She sank back to the floor and folded her legs. Surely, Sonny Mooney knew she was Zander Taylor's daughter. She turned the photo over and read the list of names on the back.

A door slammed downstairs, and she waited for Jace so she could tell him what she found. Maybe he could make sense of this.

The footsteps made the floor creak as he approached. Fergie glanced up. But instead of Jace, a strange man that she had never seen before entered the attic. She scrambled to her feet, but not fast enough.

His gaze connected with hers. She recognized him as the man who'd been in the back of the van who had killed Fritz. A small scar marked his cheek and acne scarred his face.

"Who are you?" she yelled.

"You should've left everything alone, darling." He chuckled and lifted his gun.

She grabbed for her gun, but the man turned his weapon on Fergie. He blocked her path to the door.

"Drop it, Ms. Taylor."

She swallowed. She couldn't take the chance that he might

shoot Fergie. Her hand released her weapon. At the same time, she shouted, "Fergie, retreat!"

Before he could react, she shoved the man out of the way and fled for the attic window. With a jerk, the pane slammed open, and she climbed onto the roof.

"Stop!"

But she didn't listen. She leaped to the first-story roof. The pitch was too steep, and her boots slid down the shingles and off the roof. She landed on her feet and fell forward. Just as bullets kicked dirt all around, she scrambled to her feet, and sprinted in a zigzag pattern. She screamed, "Jace!"

Bullets continued to fly, forcing her to bolt for a nearby field. She didn't even stop to turn to see if Fergie had made it to the truck. She had to believe her dog had listened to her command to retreat.

She was running so fast she almost fell but caught herself and picked up speed again. The ground was rough from the recent rains, but the tall grass was just yards in front of her. Dirt kicked up in front of her once again as the whiz of a bullet urged her on. She dove into the tall grass and rolled.

Bullets peppered all around her, but she continued to roll and then crawled through the pasture. After a few more feet, she came to a scraggly bush and got up. While staying low, she took off again. She heard the gunfire once more, but the aim was off. In the distance, Fergie barked. *Please, Jace, get her before the unknown man does.*

Jace hurried out of the barn when he heard the gunfire. Fergie was barking up a storm and a man jogged out of the Mooney house carrying a rifle. Jace pointed his weapon at the man and yelled, "Drop it."

But the man fired his weapon, and Jace retreated. The man's gun was much bigger than his own.

Lieutenant Dotson suddenly pulled up and the gunman disappeared behind the house. Dotson slammed on his brakes and jumped out of his vehicle. "Was that gunfire?"

"Yeah. The guy went behind the house. That way." Jace pointed. "He was shooting at Brynne."

The lieutenant took off. Jayce hurried over to Fergie and rubbed his hand over her head. "Come on, girl."

He needed to find Brynne before the man did. He put the Saint Bernard in the back seat of his truck. He didn't want to get in the lieutenant's way, but he also was not going to leave Brynne on her own. She had run in the opposite direction of his ranch. She was either petrified and trying to get away, or she didn't want to lead the gunman to Jace's home, to where his family was.

He could have driven fast across the grassy pasture, but he didn't want to lead the gunman straight to her. When he got to the other side of the house, he saw Lieutenant Dotson's truck flying across the field. There were several washes throughout the place, and he hoped he did not get his vehicle stuck. The gunman turned and fired several rounds at the lieutenant.

A few seconds later, they were out of sight. Jace wanted to go around and get in front of them, so he took the road and flew south. If she continued to run in a straight line, he should intersect her path. He grabbed his cell phone and tried calling her number.

She picked up on the first ring. "Jace." She sounded out of breath and attempted to whisper. "I'm trying to remain quiet."

"I'm taking the road around. Are you still going in the same direction?"

"I believe so." Her breathing sounded like it evened out, like she had stopped for a moment. "Is Fergie okay?"

"Yeah. She's with me."

"Thank goodness. Jace, he's the one who killed Fritz. I recognized him."

"Okay, I hear you. I will find you before he does. You got that?"

"Got it. And please hurry."

Jace disconnected and approached his turn. He skidded through the curve and then took off again on the rock road. His heart raced as he hoped to beat the killer to Brynne. Fergie looked out of the window, almost like she understood something was about to happen. A minute later, he slowed and searched for signs of Brynne. Dead grass blew in the chilly wind, and somebody's hand shot up about fifty yards away. He hit the brakes and threw the truck into Park. Brynne climbed to her feet and dashed across the pasture toward him. After she crossed the barbed wire fence, she fell into his arms.

"Thank you. Thank you, Jace."

"I'm glad you're okay." He looked into her eyes before pulling her into a hug. Several seconds ticked by as he breathed in the scent of her, relieved she wasn't hurt. Finally, he pulled away. "Let's go. We can talk about this when we're safe." She got in on the passenger side while he ran around and jumped into the truck.

Brynne's arms immediately went around Fergie as she gave her a hug. "I'm so glad she's safe."

Jace drove around the large country block, and then headed back toward town. He got on the highway after not seeing any sign of their attacker.

Brynne held her hand in the air. "I'm still shaking."

He reached across and grabbed her hand into his. This time she didn't pull away.

"Jace," she said, her voice softening.

He waited for her to finish her thoughts.

"I need to ask you something. And I only want the truth."

"Okay."

"Did you know Sonny was in the military with my dad?"

"No, I didn't. If I would've known that then I would have told you." As he searched her eyes, he tried to determine if she believed him.

"Then I have got to believe that Sonny knows exactly what is going on. I think it's time we follow Sonny to see what he has been up to."

"I'm on it."

SEVENTEEN

Brynne watched Sonny get out of his vehicle with her binoculars. "I see him."

Jace said, "Is he just standing there?"

"Yeah," she whispered. "He looks like he's waiting for someone."

Jace moved a little closer—so close that she could feel the heat against her shoulder.

"I'm telling you he knows something big or is deep in this. I'm just glad we caught him before he left his house so we could follow him. This warehouse is only three miles from the ranch, but us kids were always told to stay away."

"The No Trespassing signs and the three-foot block wall that surrounds the place probably helped."

"It did. I don't know what, but I think we're going to find out soon."

"I'm ready to learn the truth, but I hope Sonny is not guilty of any other crimes."

Brynne didn't respond, for she didn't feel like she could trust anyone aside from Jace and his family. But if Sonny knew something that could help her, she didn't know why he didn't say so. Someone had tried to kill her. If there was ever a time he should tell her what's going on, it was now. But he had remained quiet. It made her sick to her stomach to think the man that she thought of as a father figure could stand by while Carrie was killed, and Brynne was targeted.

Time ticked by and the wind blew through the grass, reminding Brynne why she loved the country life. If there were no worries, no danger, no one trying to kill her, she would have thought what a beautiful winter day. Fergie moved beside her, crawling on her belly, until she was directly beside Brynne. And when they were done here, she and Fergie would go back to their life in Pepper Creek. The thought made her sad, but they would get by. They always had.

Her cell phone vibrated. Sergeant Lancaster was calling. She answered. "This is Brynne."

"I thought you would want to know. We visited with Mark Stowe, the representative."

"Yeah?" Her heart picked up pace. Jace stared at her, evidently waiting to hear the news.

"After an hour of denials, he finally admitted to having an affair with Carrie back when she interned for him. But he adamantly denies having harmed her. Being that he was thirty-two years old and had a wife and a young child at the time, he begged her to put the child up for adoption and not tell anyone he was the father. He also confessed to agreeing to pay her $10,000 to help pay for her expenses once she moved out on her own if she promised not to tell. He claims to have been in Austin meeting with lawmakers on the night of her disappearance. His story checked out."

"Thank you for letting me know." When she disconnected, she quietly recounted the information to Jace.

"That eliminates Reagan's biological dad as the killer."

"Yeah. Looks like it. That means it's even more important we find out what Sonny knows." Brynne kept an eye on her foster dad while he leaned against his car and looked into the distance. Finally, he put a phone to his ear.

"Looks like he got a phone call."

"We need to keep an eye on him and not let him get away."

Sonny stuffed his phone back into his pocket and got into his car.

"He's on the move."

"Let's go." Jace hurried around Brynne's truck and climbed in on the passenger side. But as Brynne was going to climb in, she noticed Sonny just sat there at the metal shed instead of driving away. "Wait a minute. He's not leaving."

He moved his car around the back of the metal building and got out of his vehicle. He disappeared into the abandoned warehouse.

"Let's go. Come, Fergie." The dog was ready to work.

Jace showed up at her side and whispered, "We need to be careful because we have no idea what or who we're going to find."

No one had to tell her that. Her heart raced with anticipation as they skirted wide so that if anyone was looking out the window or watching the place, hopefully they would still be undercover. They moved along the tree line, staying low and moving cautiously. The wind blew and birds sang from the bare treetops.

Up ahead were several thick bushes, and she made certain they went through the middle, so as not to be spotted by anyone and to keep their presence unknown.

As they moved through the underbrush, a deep voice came from behind them. "I wished you would not have come, Brynne."

She whirled around. Jace whipped out his gun. Brynne's throat went dry, and her eyes could not believe what she was seeing.

The tall figure was all dressed in black. "Put that gun away, son."

Jace was quick to respond. "I'll do no such thing. Identify yourself."

Brynne swallowed, and her mouth felt like cotton. "Jace, I don't know how, but this is my father, Zander Taylor. Keep your gun on him." Even as the words poured from her mouth, it wasn't real. Her daddy was dead, killed in a car wreck over twenty years ago. Confusion was quickly replaced with anger. "How could you make me believe you were dead? Why are you here? Are you the one that was trying to kill me?"

"Of course not." The man sighed. "Please put the gun down."

Jace glanced at Brynne, and when she didn't argue, he holstered the gun. He moved close to her, and she was barely aware of his hand touching hers.

She wanted an explanation. But she had already asked the question, and she was afraid to try to speak again for fear of the emotion clogging her throat.

"Let's go inside." He nodded, indicating the warehouse Sonny had just entered.

"I don't think so." Her voice came out strong even though she felt anything but. "You owe me an explanation. Now."

Dark, almost black, eyes stared back at her. Her father looked older with gray-tinted hair. He still looked to be in good physical shape, though. "You're right, Brynne-Brynne. But let's not stand out here and talk about it. It's too dangerous."

"Do not call me Brynne-Brynne again," she said with an even voice. "That is an endearment I don't want to hear. How could you let a little girl believe her daddy had died when it's evident he had not?" Her hands shook as if the passion within her would boil over. She had never hated anyone in her life before, except maybe her stepdad when he hit her. But now, looking at her father, it was like he had taken a knife and stabbed her in the heart and twisted it—the pain was unbearable. And he had known she had gone into foster care, yet he hadn't come to save her. What kind of father could be so cruel?

"I will not call you that again," he said, and his voice softened. "We are in danger. I am truly sorry. Everything I did was to protect you." He pointed to the warehouse again. "Please, I'm begging you. We are too exposed."

She exchanged glances with Jace, who gave her a slight nod. "Okay."

They wound their way through the brush toward the warehouse, allowing Zander to lead them. She could not think of him as her father right now. He had betrayed her.

Traitor.

She needed the anger to return, for tears threatened. She blinked them back.

Zander opened the door while she and Fergie and Jace entered the building. He glanced over his shoulder one last time before he shut the door behind them.

Surprise appeared on Sonny's face when they entered the open space. The room was small but there were shelves on the far wall that contained what appeared to be a large assortment of ammunition. On the other wall was a cot and an old dresser that stood at the end. Above the bed were several monitors, where evidently a person could see a 360-degree view of the location. Each wall contained a window. She assumed it was so the person inside could look outside. Or maybe it was to shoot from.

"Nice bunker. How long have you had this place, Daddy?" She said the last word with sarcasm.

"I've had it for twenty years."

It didn't take long for his answer to sink in. "You watched me? While I was at the Mooney house?"

"He didn't watch you exactly," Sonny said. "He purposely pulled some strings and had you moved to my house, Brynne. It was for your own safety."

"My safety?" That made no sense, and she was tempted to accuse them of lying but she held her tongue. "Why would I be in danger? I was just a kid."

Her dad kept his distance. "Because of me. I have been in witness protection for years, not long after I left your mother… I turned evidence against a crooked judge and two lawyers. I was doing landscape work at Judge Talman's house when I overheard him accept a bribe to throw a case with a dangerous drug lord. I came forward as an informant if the police agreed to keep my identity a secret. However, my identity was leaked by someone in the police department who was under the judge's payroll. After my testimony, the judge was convicted, but he had ties to criminals and a variety of crooked people in the system. They wanted to take me out. When they could not find me, they killed my army buddy, Travis Petty."

For some reason, Brynne remembered that name. How did she know it? That's it. It was from the third photo. His name was written on the back of the photo of his squad.

He continued, "I had kept an eye on you and your mother. Your mother and I were not getting along so I had already left her before the judge sent a man after me. But when they killed Petty, I knew they would stop at nothing to get me to come out of hiding. I did the only thing I could. I faked my death and went off the grid in Montana for a few years. When I learned you had been put into foster care, I called an old friend, a senator, who pulled strings to have you moved into the Mooney home. I trusted Sonny could keep you safe."

This was all surreal. She was still having a hard time understanding everything. She still had a lot of questions.

"Then why did somebody attack me? Correction. Why did someone kill Carrie?"

Jace jumped in. "If the judge and lawyers believed you were dead, there would be no reason to target Brynne."

All three people turned to him. Zander looked him over slowly.

Zander said, "Exactly. I've kept my eye on you, Jace Jackson. Like I said, I stayed off the grid for several years, got a new identity and laid low. Michael Mueller, another army buddy, gave me a call one day. I went to see him because he thought something illegal was going on, and he wanted help from someone he could trust. I met with him, and he told me about suspicious activity concerning arms deals. He thought someone was trying to frame him for it."

Distrust still championed her thoughts. She said, "Why would he ask you? How did he even know you were alive?"

He gave her a look, showing he wasn't used to being questioned. But he answered her, anyway. "There were a handful of people I stayed in contact with. People I knew I could trust. People I could call on if I ever got in trouble and needed protection. They felt the same about me. There were places I could stay and not be spotted."

"Like this bunker?" she asked.

"Yeah, like this bunker. It's not safe for people like me to stay in hotels or rented rooms. Not if I have other options."

That meant he probably stayed here often enough to invest in the bunker. She didn't know if that made her feel better because he cared, or angry that he didn't try to form a relationship with her when she was so close. Growing up had been hard, and a father's love would've made a huge difference.

"Anyway," he continued, "after he met with me, he was killed. Shot execution-style. The problem was I had a cup of coffee while I was there. The police found my DNA. It didn't take long for the lawyers to figure out I was still alive. From the intel I have gathered, Fritz was supposed to kidnap you to bring me out in the open. But you and Carrie looked alike enough, and evidently, he had been watching the place. When he saw you drop the baby off at the fire station, he believed you were Carrie, and vice versa. When she put up a fight, he killed her."

It was like a punch to the gut. All this time, it was Brynne who should have been attacked. Carrie was innocent. She had nothing to do with anything. A young life snuffed out simply because someone believed she was Brynne. "How did you learn all this information?"

"I have my sources."

Brynne stared at him for several moments. She still couldn't grasp that he was alive. It was like watching a movie play out in front of her. Except instead of actors, she was the one in the story, and she didn't want to be there. She wanted to go back in time and erase the awful nightmare she was living. "I have just one more question."

"What's that?"

"Who are you?" As he stared at her, she went on. "What do you do for a living? How do you support yourself? And how could you learn all these things?"

"Some things you are better off not knowing."

"You owe me an explanation."

But before their discussion could continue, Sonny said, "We have company."

Her dad grabbed a rifle and Sonny already had one in his hands. Brynne swallowed hard. She didn't even know who these gunmen were or why they were after her daddy. She glanced at Jace, and she felt nothing but numbness. Jace had simply tried to help her, and now he was deep over his head. This was her fault, not his. And he was the daddy of that precious child.

Please, Lord, help us get out of this situation. Jace is innocent, and if You have to choose only one, keep him safe.

Jace read the hurt on Brynne's face, and it took everything within him not to intervene between her and her father. How could any man let her daughter believe he was dead? He grabbed her by the hand and led her to the back of the bunker to a small kitchen area. "We need to get out of here."

"No. We need to stand against these men. We can sort this out when it's over. And if my father must go to jail then he goes to jail. I've never had him in my life, anyway. What difference would it make?"

Jace knew she did not mean that. Not when the danger was over, she would not be okay with her father not being in her life again. But there was no need to have that discussion now. The main thing was to get them out of here or to take down the gunmen.

Brynne retrieved the gun from her holster. Although it seemed inadequate compared to the firepower of her dad and Sonny. She moved beside her old foster dad as he looked out the window on the north side, feeling that he was a safer option than Zander. "How many men are out there?"

"I've seen three, but don't bet your life on there not being several more." How many people could they hold off? When Brynne stepped back from the window, Jace moved next to her and whispered, "Have you notified the lieutenant or the sheriff?"

"Not the sheriff. Lieutenant Dotson was at the Mooney home when I fled. I messaged him I was okay after you picked me up, but I haven't heard back. I told Sergeant Lancaster we were following Sonny."

"You must let them know our location, Brynne. Your dad can stand on his own."

"I know that."

He watched the monitors for a few seconds and saw a man run across the drive with something in his hand. Then the guy took off, sprinting back for cover, but his hands were empty. Before he made it to cover, Zander opened fire. The man fell, got back to his feet and dove into the trees.

Boom! The door blew off at hinges and the ground shook. But the building remained standing.

Jace swallowed hard. He didn't like being locked down again. They had already gone through this in the old church building, and he had no desire for a repeat. Fergie stood next to Brynne. She watched the Saint Bernard with concern in her eyes.

"You've got to let them know, Brynne. It's the right thing." He could see by her expression that she agreed with him but hated to do it.

Sonny said, "Jace, watch for me."

He observed the monitors as Sonny moved to the other side of the room and looked out another window. From what Jace could see, there were no more attempts from the assailants to come for the bunker with Zander standing by the open door. He fired off a couple more shots. Whether he actually saw someone, or it was just a warning, Jace didn't know.

He only half listened to Brynne talk to the sheriff and his heart went out to her. He knew her career and her life were on the line. And he knew Brynne. She would not willingly give up Fergie. He looked back over his shoulder at her and saw her disconnect and put her phone away. He waited but she did not say anything to him.

He nodded toward Sonny, and she gave him the okay nod.

He had his gun in his hand and whispered, "Sonny, what do you want me to do?"

"Just stay out of the way."

Jace might have known. He had worked for Sonny for years, and as far as he knew, the man had always respected him. But when it came to guns in a shootout, the old army soldier kicked in.

Brynne got Jace's attention and told him to come there. He did as she asked. "What did the sheriff say?"

"They are on their way, but he's not happy. I'm sure he believes I'm more trouble than I'm worth."

"That's not true. None of this is your fault. Just do your job like you always do."

Her voice lowered. "I have a plan. I don't imagine either my dad or Sonny will agree. But they are not the only ones who are trained in law enforcement. And Fergie is a very well-trained canine."

Before she could continue, Zander yelled out, "The skinny guy has moved to number three."

Brynne whispered. "What is number three?"

Jace looked at the security monitors. Black boxes hung on the block wall about every twenty to thirty feet. "Look there. The boxes. Do you see them?"

"Yeah."

Sonny held a small electronic device in his hand. "Let me know when."

"Wait," Brynne yelled. "What are you doing?"

"Stay out of the way," Zander said.

She stepped up. "No. You can't just kill these men. I'm in law enforcement. We at least need to try to take them in so they can stand trial."

"Girl, these men are professionals." Sonny narrowed his gaze. "Do as your daddy says."

"No," she said again. "If those are explosives, denotate one as a distraction. I'll run out the back door and come in behind them."

Zander stared at her. "I don't want to lose you. Not again."

"It's not your choice."

"That's taking a big chance," Sonny argued.

"Do what she says," Zander said to Sonny. "Hit number five, wait three seconds and hit number eight. I'll go out the front."

Sonny clenched his jaw but gave an affirmative nod.

Jace moved beside Brynne and waited at the back door. She commanded Fergie to stay.

"On the count of three. One. Two Three."

Brynne slung the door open, just as an explosion flashed. Jace raced along with her to the corner of the warehouse just as another blast shook. With guns in their grip, they made it to the block wall.

That's when he saw the sheriff's SUV pull into the yard and Dotson get out, along with Jeff and Boss.

The man who'd killed Fritz was hunkered down and taking aim at Zander.

"Drop it," Brynne shouted. "Sheriff's department."

The skinny man spun with his gun up.

Brynne fired and hit the ground. Jace was beside her and was ready in case the man tried to shoot again.

Three more shots came from somewhere, but Jace and Brynne had taken cover.

Suddenly, a fast German shepherd sprinted across the yard and jumped on the skinny man, his teeth sinking into the man's arm. The guy screamed and fell to the ground until Jeff called Boss off.

Brynne got up and made her way across the yard. When she came up to the skinny guy, she held her gun on him until Lieutenant Dotson slapped handcuffs on the man and got him to his feet.

Jace moved up beside her. "Well done, Taylor."

"Thanks." She smiled.

As the lieutenant and Jeff hauled the assailants toward the sheriff's vehicle, Jace looked for Sonny and Zander.

That's when he saw Sonny on the ground with red on his sleeve. "Sonny's hurt."

"Oh, no," Brynne gasped. They hurried over as the man tried to get to his feet.

Zander grabbed Sonny's uninjured arm and helped him up. "We're getting too old for this."

"I'm as fit as I ever was," Sonny growled.

Brynne's dad laughed. "I'd like you to explain that to your wife."

"Oh, she's not going to be happy."

Sheriff Loughlin walked over to their group. "We have paramedics on the way. Sonny, you need to sit down. I don't want you passing out on us."

Jace laughed as Sonny started complaining.

The sheriff looked at Zander. "You Zander Taylor?" At his nod, the sheriff continued. "I'll need you to come by the department. We need to discuss how you tie in to all this."

Zander nodded. "It's time."

Brynne's expression had grown serious as she looked at the sheriff. Jace moved beside her for support. "Boss did good. I know you'd probably prefer to have another German shepherd or Belgian Malinois on the team. But Fergie…"

Sheriff Loughlin held up his hand. "Taylor, Boss is a superb canine at apprehending. Like I said, we're a team, and you're a part of that team. Fergie is a competent SAR dog, and the best in Texas with comforting the victim, for a Saint Bernard or any other breed. I'll see you on Monday."

Jace stepped back to give them room. The gunmen were apprehended. Now what? He didn't want his relationship with Brynne to end. He grabbed her hand. "We need to talk."

"Jace, you don't owe me anything. I appreciate everything you've done and for being at my side." She pulled her hand away. "I'll give you a ride home."

"That's not necessary." He'd call Sam to come pick him up.

"Okay. I'm sure I'll see you around."

He watched as she disappeared into the warehouse, emptiness descending on him.

Tears brimmed in her eyes as she attached Fergie's leash to her harness. She walked out of the warehouse and as they passed Jace, Fergie whimpered, trying to go to him.

"Come on, girl," she mumbled. She loaded Fergie into her truck. As she backed out, she tried not to look at Jace, but she couldn't help one glance. He didn't appear happy, either. She turned on the road toward her home.

The sheriff had let her know her job was secure with the department. She solved Carrie's murder. Carrie's killer was dead and the ones who assassinated Fritz were in custody. Her daddy was alive, and the authorities would be working to extend the prison term for the judge who targeted him.

Then why was she miserable?

She'd never intended to reconnect with Jace. He'd broken his promise to her.

He apologized. And he explained why.

Then why was she so certain she didn't want to have anything to do with him? Thirty minutes later, she pulled into her drive no happier than she'd been when she left the warehouse scene. Instead of a welcoming and warm home like before, her house felt empty and cold. The colored pillows on the couch were too clean…unused. No mess made by children. No laughter or loud voices.

Fergie lay down on her bed and whimpered.

"I know, girl. It's too quiet."

Suddenly a loud knock on the door made her jump. She hurried to the front door and looked in the peephole. Jace stood there with his arms folded across his chest.

She opened the door. "Did you forget something?"

"No, let me in. We need to talk. I'm not going to let you go again."

She shook her head. "You don't owe me anything. You heard the sheriff. I'm going to have a job here for a long time and hopefully he'll help make sure the judge will be prosecuted for paying others to target my dad."

"I said, I'm not going to let you go." His dark eyes connected with hers. "Trust in me."

She wanted to believe in him. She truly did. But could she take the chance? With a swing of her hand, she motioned for him to come in.

He stepped into the living room and stopped in the middle of the floor. He stared at the tile as if gathering his thoughts. Somehow the space dwindled with him standing there.

Fergie didn't get up from her bed, but her tail slapped the rug as she watched him.

When Brynne started to speak, he held his finger up, stopping her. He looked at her. "People have given you reason to not believe in them. My biggest regret is being one of those who caused you to doubt. I should've done what my heart told me to do when you were moved to West Texas and went after you. Even though we hadn't dated because I felt you were too young at the time, I had made a promise to you. I'm sorry I broke my word. There's nothing worse than to be hurt by those you care about."

Sincerity danced in his eyes. Yes, Brynne believed Jace understood. As much as she cared for him, a niggle of fear churned in her stomach. "But what if…"

"No what ifs."

He pulled her close and kissed her forehead. "We won't know until we try. I have Huck to think about. I don't take relationships lightly."

She drew away. "I'm fine on my own."

"Not good enough. I've missed you." He planted a light kiss on her lips and pulled her closer. "Don't you get it? I love you, Brynne. I always have. But if you really want me to walk away, I'll respect that."

"You love me?" A smile came to her lips as she reveled in his embrace and wrapped her arms around his neck.

It was all the encouragement he needed. He cupped her chin with his hand. And this time when he pressed his lips to hers, she kissed him back. His gentle touch felt like a promise of tomorrow.

She said, "I love you, too."

EPILOGUE

Eighteen months later...

Huck held a fishing pole as he ran up to Jace with Fergie trotting alongside him. "I caught one, I caught one."

Brynne looked up just in time to see Jace chuckle. "You sure did. That's a big one."

She had to smile. The fish couldn't be over four inches long, not that it mattered. Huck was still just as excited as he could be. The boy loved Fergie and the two were inseparable.

Reagan smiled. "I love watching them."

"Me, too. I'm so glad you can spend the day with us." Brynne adjusted her lawn chair, which sat under the carport shade and again sipped on her lemonade. It was amazing how much Reagan looked like Carrie. She enjoyed coming out to the ranch to ride horses and hear stories about her mother. What was even more amazing was that Brynne enjoyed telling the stories. It made her realize how life had its ups and downs, but things were never all bad. Nor were they all good. But everyone could make the best out of what they were given.

Her dad hollered from the yard. "Jace, how do you like your steak?"

Jace yelled back, "Medium well."

Her dad already knew what she and Reagan preferred. Jace's mom had not returned to Mississippi last year, like Jace had figured. Instead, after Brynne and Jace married a year ago, she decided she wanted to live around her grandkids. Twice a year she went for a couple of weeks to care for her mother and spend time with her sisters. Jace's grandmother was ninety-one years old and in fair condition for a woman of her age.

Sam and Tessa visited often, and their family played games together. Last year, when she and Jace married, Brynne would have never been able to picture her being surrounded by so many friends and loved ones. It was what she had always dreamed of, and some of the people she felt she had lost years ago were now in her life again. It was said that God worked in mysterious ways. The words weren't written in scripture, but she thought she understood the meaning. It was something Brynne felt. She and Fergie still worked for the sheriff's department and just last month she helped find a man with dementia who had wandered away from his home. Not all the stories had happy endings, but she enjoyed being able to rescue people if she was able. Their baby was due in September. Both agreed they did not want to know the gender but wanted to be surprised. Huck wanted a brother. Neither she nor Jace had a preference.

Her dad was now working in security and was no longer in witness protection. He was good at security and was a natural at surveillance after being in the army. Judge Talman faced trial this past January and was found guilty of murder for hire. Ninety-nine years was added to his original twenty-year prison sentence.

Jace approached her and kissed her cheek. "You look beautiful, babe."

"You always say that." She smiled. He looked good, too.

She had always had a thing for cowboys. Still did. But with Reagan sitting there she wasn't going to say anything.

She often thought of how nice it would be if Carrie could be with her and see her daughter. She was thankful for Reagan's adoptive parents and thought Carrie would be happy the couple had provided a loving home to Carrie's baby, and Reagan was very close to that family. But it warmed Brynne's heart to know Reagan didn't hold ill feelings toward her birth mother who gave her up, nor Brynne, who had dropped her off at a fire station many years ago.

Brynne felt the baby kick, and she knew she would do everything in the world to protect the little one. And looking at Reagan, she guessed in her own way she had done that many years ago. Jace winked at her. His beautiful eyes and crooked smile made her heart flip. She said, "Love you, babe."

"Right back at you."

* * * * *

If you liked this story from Connie Queen, check out her previous Love Inspired Suspense books:

Justice Undercover
Texas Christmas Revenge
Canyon Survival
Abduction Cold Case
Tracking the Tiny Target
Rescuing the Stolen Child
Wilderness Witness Survival

Available now from Love Inspired Suspense!

Find more great reads at LoveInspired.com.

Dear Reader,

Thank you for joining me on Jace and Brynne's journey. And Fergie, too!

In every story, I try to find at least one unique element in the crime or setting. This time I added a baptistry in the floor of the pulpit. When I was young, our building had one like I describe in the story. As kids, we were also told to stay away and not lift the door for obvious reasons. I searched images on the internet and could only find one out of hundreds. Yes, one. That made me wonder if it was a regional thing. What about you? Are you familiar with the baptistry hidden under a trapdoor in the pulpit?

I love hearing from readers! You can connect with me at www.conniequeenauthor.com on my Facebook page.

Connie Queen